OUT THERE BAD

A Moses McGuire Novel

By Josh Stallings

Copyright © 2011 Josh Stallings

All rights reserved under International and Pan-American Copyright Conventions.

Published in the United States by Heist Publishing

ISBN: 978-0615497853

WWW.JOSHSTALLINGS.NET

DEDICATION

For Fiona Johnson. As fierce a champion as any war tattered old bouncer and his equally tore-up creator could hope for.

ACKNOWLEDGMENTS

Without these folks there would be no book... Erika for countless hours of reading and re-reading my work, and always loving me enough to tell me when it totally sucks. The dancers of Cheetahs, Star Strip Too and Fantasy Island who take their clothes off and bare more than their breasts. Jared and Dylan for sharing my life and teaching me how to be a dad. Larkin Stallings, brother and running mate. Lisa Stallings who told me I should take Moses out of the drawer and put him into the world. My little sister Shaun Anzaldua, an early reader and true friend. My mother and father for instilling the love of a good story. Julie Lewthwaite who helped Erika cross my t's and dot my i's. Charlie Huston for his continued support and belief in me. Tad Williams and Deborah Beale, who again generously shared their editorial knowledge, time, coffee and boundless friendship. Elizabeth A. White, Paul D. Brazill, Sabrina E. Ogden and all my other online friends who helped Moses stumble into the world. Thank you all from the depths of my heart.

CHAPTER 1

MEXICO CITY - AUGUST 14TH 6:26 PM

Central slave market. Hunting. No leads to Russian girls yet. Yesterday a young man told me he could take me to a stable of Russian whores. He lied. He tried to rob me. I slit his throat. Left a tarot card on his chest. Left his body in the gutter. One more piece of trash to be picked up.

I travel light, everything I need fits in my coat. Russian military issue. The soldier who owned it won't need it to keep warm anymore.

Down a fresh alley. Deeper into the labyrinth. Broken hollow-faced girls stare out of the shadows. Olive skin, brown eyes. Broken. I must keep on point. Solve what I came to solve. Fight for all and you will win none. Simple math. Men laugh. Men drink. Men step out of the way when they see me coming. They can smell death.

"Tell me where the Russian girls are?"

"Fuck if I know, maybe here, maybe there. How much money you got?" He is a middleman. He thinks he is in control because we are in his office. Outside a closed door are three armed men. He feels safe.

The razor is so fast his little finger is off before he can scream. My hand clamps down on his mouth. The blade rests against his throat. Blood is leaking from the stub on his hand. His eyes are huge. "Where are the Russian girls?"

He hesitates. A second finger is gone. He screams into my gloved hand.

"Where?" He nods. His eyes plead. I slowly pull my hand from his mouth. The blade rests on his throat.

"Norte, Baja maybe. Rumors. Don't kill me."

"No Russian girls here?"

"No, I swear, I only tell the truth. Please."

I step behind him. I arc down. His throat gushes. His only sound is a gurgling moan. I hold his mouth closed. Then he is dead. I drop a tarot card on his body. His three men will die. They will have cards on their bodies.

LOS ANGELES - AUGUST 14TH 8:32 PM

"Moses, let me give you a lap dance, baby." Caramel was a big-boned, light-skinned black girl, with mountains of frizzy sun-bleached hair. She wore thigh high Vampira boots and a black leather thong with a matching leather bra so small it barely covered her nipples. If I was any other man, I'd have had to wipe buckets of drool off my chin as she crawled on my lap. But I was me, the bouncer, doing time in titty daycare.

"Little boy, you know you want some of this candy, you know you got a sweet-tooth for Caramel."

"I don't do that anymore, baby girl," I said.

"Ha!"

"Really."

"Why not?" She reached over to stroke my lap. I didn't pull away, no need insulting her... besides, I'm not a saint and her touch felt good. It was a slow night, two Mexican boys sat at the bar trying to get up the courage to move down to the stage.

With no one at the stage to tip, the girls weren't dancing. Instead, they sat on the leopard-print sofas, gossiping and getting drunk. Slow nights can be a lot more dangerous than busy ones. Bored, drunk strippers rip it up when the mood hits them wrong.

"That skinny bitch done broke your heart and turned you into a monk?" Caramel purred into my ear. "You used to be all into this fine ass." I was starting to swell under her attention. "Come on, let me give you a down low nasty call-the-Vice-Squad dance."

"Can't. Want to, can't."

"I think the girls are right. You pitching for the other team?"

"Maybe."

"Oh, come on, Moses, you ain't gay. Your point man is standing up ready for combat."

"What's the pot up to?"

"What are you talking about, baby?"

"You're not tossing me a freebee 'cause I'm cute. Sure isn't my massive wealth. How much is the bet up to?" She looked at me, fighting to find a quick lie, but it wouldn't come fast enough. "Fifty? A hundred?"

"Moses, it wasn't like-"

"Bullshit. Nothing happens in here I don't know about. Sadie or China is holding a bag full of your hard-earned cash. First girl to get me in the back room wins the pot. Tell me I'm wrong."

"Will you believe me?" She looked down at the table.

"No. You girls think I'm here to amuse you? Let's see who can get Moses all hot and bothered, then laugh about it in the dressing room... Fuck it." I stood up and walked away before she could tell me how damn sorry she was.

I banged out the back door and onto the landing of the steep steel stairs that led down thirty feet to the parking lot below. I leaned on the safety-rail, sucking in what stood for fresh air in August, in the city of broken angels. City of wild, damaged dreams and beautiful graffiti-splashed cement rivers. LA, where nothing is what it seems on the surface and everybody lies about what's underneath. Guys here drive $174,000 German sports cars, then argue over a twenty dollar cover charge and tip a naked girl a buck to put her tits in his face. This city is morally mortgaged to the hilt and drowning in the vig. Three decades after the riots of '92 and they had learned nothing, nothing at all. Separation between rich and poor, wider than ever, a true feudal system where lowly serfs like me get by on what they toss down, or what we can scam off them through their need for vice.

"Hey, Cowboy." Piper walked out onto the balcony. At near thirty, she was considered the old lady of Club Xtasy, but could out dance and out sell any of the eighteen year old shakers in the club. Flame red hair cascaded down, framing her face in its fire. She had a tall tight body topped off with a rack that would make a schoolboy give up his paper route money for one brief touch.

"You thinking of jumping?" She looked over the edge of the stairs, tilting her head in a brief nod.

"Over some stripper bullshit? I don't think so."

"It was just a joke, Mo. They're bored."

"Fuck them. Next time some freak has his hand up their ass, maybe I'll look the other way. How's that for a funny fucking joke."

"You won't."

"Why the hell not, huh? One reason."

"Didn't say you shouldn't. Said you won't. You're not wired that way. Which is one of the coolest things about you, big man. That and your fine ass." She reached out, dancing her finger across the back of my jeans.

I jerked away. "What, you need the cash that bad? Here." Pulling a hundred out of my pocket, I tossed it at her.

"Fuck you, Moses." She let the bill fall. "Have a drink, get laid, whatever it takes. The way you are now, it's getting really hard to care about you." Her eyes were wet, but she'd never cry, she was a pro. She spun and clicked her way back into the club.

It had been fourteen months since the last time I had played Russian roulette, six months since my last dose of speed, three weeks since my last drink and ten minutes since my last deadly thought. Why? I hadn't quit drinking and drugging and letting girls friction-fuck me out of some moral stance. I quit it because none of it was working anymore. All it did was make me feel sad and empty. Before Cass left me she taught me what it felt like to be touched by a woman who really wanted me, just for being me. I had known what it felt like to be loved, or the best approximation of love two children of the battle zone could muster. Maybe she came to me because I was a big man and could protect her, maybe it was gratitude for saving her life and taking out the punk who killed her sister, or maybe it was simply that her scars fit with mine. I didn't care why, she was mine and I was hers. It didn't last, it couldn't, but for a time it had felt real and when she left me, I knew I was through settling for fake passion.

Before Cass, I could pretend that these strippers I kept safe might actually have wanted a sliced up, tattered old warhorse like me. The trouble is, once you know you're telling yourself a lie, it stops working. My odometer was going to click over to forty-four in October, I guess it was time I started telling the truth, if only to myself.

I was heading back in when I noticed a red Porsche down in the lot. Big buck rides almost never park in the back. We don't valet, we don't patrol, like the sign says, PARK AT YOUR OWN RISK. The street in front of the club is better lit and there's enough traffic to keep it reasonably safe. Staring hard through the sunroof I could make out the driver. His hands were laced into a woman's platinum blond hair. He roughly forced her head down onto his lap.

I moved down the stairs with as much stealth as my building rage would allow. Crossing the parking lot I could see in the Porsche's rear window. Driver's face was caught in the mirror, contorting with a mixture of anger and pleasure. He had a two hundred dollar haircut, the kind meant to look like he just crawled out of bed, and one of those stupid soul patches growing under his lower lip. Getting within a few feet, I could hear his choked muttering: "...right bitch, suck hard bitch..."

When I ripped the door open the driver's face snapped around. But instead of fear, he looked indignant. "Dude - what the fuck?" He released his grip on the platinum hair and the bobbing head shot up off his lap.

"Moses?"

"Marina." She was a new Russian dancer. I motioned with my head for her to get out.

"What the fuck, dude, she's busy, take a number."

Grabbing a fistful of his suede sports coat I dragged the driver out. His legs got tangled under the dash. I yanked hard. The leather tore. He flopped onto the pavement fighting to get his legs working. Whatever he was screaming I couldn't hear it over the blood rushing in my ears.

My fist caught him under the chin, lifting him up and bouncing him off the hood of his Porsche. I was about to smash him again -

"Moses! No, stop!" Marina was behind me, screaming. I let go. He was a kid, maybe twenty. Blood smeared his gums and teeth.

"You bwoke my fucking tooth." The swelling gave him a lisp. "My dad ith tho going to thue your ath."

Marina pushed past me. "Baby, you are ok, yes? So brave." She was cooing in the little fucker's face.

"You know him?" I asked. Stupid question, sure, but I was trying to play catch up while my pulse rocked adrenaline into my tiny brain.

"Fuck yeth, she knowth me. I just paid her fifty to polith my knob." Standing up, he zipped his pants closed.

"You paid her for sex?"

"Yeth, you fucking deaf? - one of you owth me fifty buckth or a blow job. Not to mention a god damn tooth."

"Sex for hire is illegal, pal, I don't think you want to push it," I said over my shoulder as I walked away. I knew if I looked at him I might explode. It had been years since I had been in the joint and I didn't plan on returning, not over a creep like this.

"Tell that to your hot little thlut there, thee'th the one who offered it. I jutht went along for the ride."

"You really need to stop talking," I said soft. Still turned with my back to him, I stopped walking. I felt my muscles tensing, they knew a dogfight was coming, even if my brain was in denial.

"Look ath wipe, your bitch took my-" I felt his hand grabbing my upper arm. His touch unleashed me, like a snapping high-tension spring I spun around. If he had more to say, I'll never know; my fist shoved his words back down his throat. The blow rocked his jaw two inches out of alignment and sent a fine spray of pink mist gracing the night air.

He was fit and gym tough, I'll give him that. He took it and threw one of his own. I ducked to the left and took his fist on the side of my head. I could hear bones in his hand snapping against my skull. Grabbing him by the ears I slammed my thick brow down. His nose went with a thick wet crunch. Blood streamed down his face. I gave him two quick shots to the gut, he doubled over gasping for air and spewing bile and blood. I was in full tilt berserker mode. No mercy asked, none given.

7

I swung my arm back, preparing to ruin his pretty boy face. A powerful hand grabbed my arm and held me back.

"It's done, Moses." Uncle Manny held my arm, staring me down. He was a good foot and a half shorter than me and fifty pounds lighter, but I'd never think of taking him on. I relaxed my muscles and formed a smile. As soon as Manny released his grip, I spun and laid my boot to the punk's chest. I heard the crack of ribs and the squeal of deep hurt.

"Moses!"

"Fine, fuck him."

The punk in the suit was curled up on the ground like a puking fetus. Uncle Manny turned to his nephew. "Turaj! Clean this up."

"But Uncle, Moses did-"

"Get him in his car and off my lot."

Turaj gave me what he hoped was a withering glance and moved over to follow his uncle's orders.

Marina stood watching us, her eyes wide with fear. She was a frozen rabbit I was the headlights on the highway. I tried to say something to her but only a low rasp came out.

Uncle Manny walked me up the stairs. He was the club's owner and one of the few older men in the world who actually trusted and respected me. He was a tough man who escaped Iran in the middle of the revolution. He watched his brother die in a firefight at the border, but against all odds, he made it to America and raised his children soft and comfortable. Insuring they would never understand him. Not the way I would.

"Sit the fuck down, you piece of shit." Through the walls of his office the dance music thumped.

"Manny, I can-"

"You can shut the fuck up. That boy sues me? I lose my club? Who pays for my kids' college? You?"

"Fuck this, Manny."

"Sit down." I did.

"I was doing my job."

"I pay you to hurt my patrons?"

"Marina was giving him a blow job."

"These things happen. Moses, think... we sell the pretense of sex, sometimes it crosses the line. Do we like that? No, but it is the cost of doing business."

We always had a zero tolerance rule about freelancing. Get caught with that crap not only will Vice take your license, they'd put someone in the can.

"We can't let that shit pass."

"Calm down. You look ready to explode. You are a hand grenade and the pin is lost."

"I'm cool."

"You don't look cool. When was the last time you got laid?"

"What?"

"When, was the last time, you got laid?"

"That's none of your business, Manny."

"Bullshit answer. Weeks? No? Months?"

"It has been a while, ok?"

"That's no good. Keep that up and you will kill one of my customers."

"He came at me, I was defending..." Even I didn't believe it.

"You, me, we can stop these boys with one word, a hard look. It's bad business, what you did."

"I'm sorry, Manny... He just, I don't know..."

"No, you don't know. I'd rather have blow jobs than killing in my parking lot." From out of his safe he took a small wad of bills and passed them across the table.

"What's this?"

"Two weeks' pay."

"Firing me?"

"For now."

"Later?"

"We'll see. Kid presses it, I need to show I took action. Now go, I have a club to run."

I was at the door when he spoke, I kept my back to him.

"You want some advice from an old man, that you didn't ask for?"

"Not really."

"Find a good woman, one not in this life, and settle down. Someone to come home to at night. Someone to grow old with. Now get out of here."

Marina stood in front of the club as I rolled up out of the parking lot. She looked small, her shoulders rounded in, draped in a too-large trench coat. Her eyes darted around. Something had her spooked.

"You ok, baby girl?" I said as I walked up to her. She shrank back into the shadows of the building. "You don't have to be afraid of me."

"No?" she said softly.

"No. I'd die before I'd smack one of you girls." She relaxed slightly; uncrossing her arms she let them drop to her side. "Uncle Manny fire you over that crap in the car?"

"Just for this night, yes, but tomorrow, no."

"He's a fair man. Listen, the BJ, is that a regular thing?"

"No. First time. I swear."

"Alright. You say it was a one shot deal, then it was a one shot deal. Why'd you do it? You know the rules, right?"

"Yes. It was slow this night. I have rent to pay." Before she could say more, a black Mercedes slid up and double parked in front of us. An S500, a couple years old, but still its driver had to be packing some major ching. Marina was already moving towards the car when she spoke. "I have to go." She climbed quickly into the back seat.

"Marina?" I stepped into the street. "If you get jammed up for cash again, come to me before you do something stupid."

"Thank-" Whatever else she had to say was lost in the noise of the Mercedes whipping away.

Everything about the black sedan rang wrong. It wasn't the car a broke girl got picked up in, and if it was a "date" she would have gotten in the front. Fucking Russians, soon as I thought I had their scams figured out, they invented new ones. They were mean, evil bastards who would slit your throat soon as look at you, but they weren't subtle.

"Do you know how to tell when a whore is lying?" an old man asked me when I was in lockdown. "Their lips are moving." He burst into a fit of laughter that almost cost him a lung.

CHAPTER 2

The red dress was the only legacy Nika's sister had left her. It was just before dawn when she pulled it over her head. The silky fabric clung tightly across her breasts. It looked good, right. These tits that appeared as an unwanted gift on her twelfth birthday had caused only trouble, they made sports awkward and brought teasing from her classmates. For the last year she had hidden her chest in baggy shirts, but seeing how she filled out her sister's dress, she was glad to have developed early. Her hips on the other hand were still like a boy's. The fabric fell from her waistline, hung loosely, losing all form. Pulling up the hem, she wrapped a winter scarf from butt to pelvis, encasing herself in the thick wool. Dropping the skirt down she checked again, smiled; she was becoming a woman. Her one pair of dress shoes were scuffed and half a size too small. The first thing she was going to buy when she got to America was a new pair of heels. Spiked, like the girls wore on MTV.

Cracking the bedroom door, Nika checked on her father. He was still passed out on the sofa that served as his bed. An empty bottle of homemade wine lay on the carpet. In the last year, he had given up the pretense of a wine glass and drank from the bottle. He had been a professor before the Ruble crashed and the Yaroslavl academy closed. Now, there was no work for a sixty year old philosophy teacher. Economics teachers, sure, but in the new Russia no one wanted philosophy.

It was time, all Nika needed was a final push. Sitting on her bed she unfolded the telegram and reread it for the hundredth time.

DEAREST VERONIKA. LIFE IN AMERICA IS WONDERFUL. I LIVE IN A LOVELY HOUSE IN LOS ANGELES. WE HAVE A POOL. YOU WILL LOVE IT HERE. I HAVE ARRANGED WITH AN EMPLOYMENT AGENT FOR YOU TO COME AND LIVE WITH ME. HE HAS FOUND YOU A JOB AT A HOTEL. DO NOT TELL FATHER OR HE WILL STOP YOU FROM COMING. WE CAN WRITE HIM ONCE YOU ARE HERE IN THE SUNSHINE. LOVE ANYA

There was a postscript with the phone number and address for the Moscow employment agency. "Veronika", her sister had called her "Veronika" instead of the childish "Nika" she had used when they were children. Anya must know she was grown now.

Nika's heart pounded. She was heading for a new life in a new land. It meant leaving school and her friends, but so what? What good was an education when doctors starved and only the Mafia got rich? Nika was chasing a dream that most in her small town never even had the courage to imagine. She was going to the land of Beverly Hills, 90210. Who knew, she might even be discovered and become a star. She could sing and dance as well as Miley Cyrus. Hadn't she won the May Day talent contest? Yes, it was clear she was too big for the small life Yaroslavl could offer. Her father would be angry, but he would forgive her when she arrived home in her chauffeur-driven limousine.

She closed the flat's door as softly as possible. Early summer had broken, melting the snow and turning the dirt to mud. Nika walked the path along the Volga River. Brave holidayers were swimming in the freezing water. The ice had only broken up a month ago, but if cold held you back, you would never swim in Yaroslavl. Two teenage boys sat up on their towels, watching her pass. Apparently they liked what they saw, they let out loud whistles and waved for her to join them. Nika was not accustomed to attention from boys of any age, but especially not from cute older boys wearing only swim suits. She felt the heat of a blush flowing up her cheeks. Turning away, she quickened her step.

Nika had a small bag slung over her shoulder, it held all she was taking with her - several pairs of threadbare cotton panties and bras, a photo of her mother taken before the cancer ruined her looks, a small stack of Rubles and the telegram. Whatever else she needed, she would buy in America.

Crossing the river on a stone bridge she looked to the old church that towered above the small shops, its gold onion domes lit fire in the morning sun. There were some things she would miss, just not many.

The train was near full when Nika climbed on. Moving past the private berths she saw well-dressed men and women lounging in style. In the coach section she searched for a seat alone, but it was Sunday and the car was packed with weekenders heading back to the city. A fat, sweaty man stuffed himself in beside her. He was reading Provda. When he thought she wasn't looking, he let his eyes flit across her body.

He licked the sweat off his upper lip and smiled a private smile. For a moment, Nika wished she had not chosen to wear her sister's dress.

No, she was starting a new life, she didn't want to go to America in her old clothes. She closed her eyes and blocked out the train car by imagining how cool life was going to be in Los Angeles. Palm trees, gated houses, swimming pools. She and Anya would get a house on a nice street and they would each have their own room. No one would have to sleep on the sofa.

The squealing of the brakes woke Nika. The Moscow station loomed monstrously around the train. At two in the morning the sun had recently set, leaving the city cloaked in streetlights and shadows.

Nika was sucked along with the other passengers as they swept through the station. At the head of the stairs leading down to the underground, she stopped, unsure of where to go. She read the subway map on the wall, but it only confused her more. She had no idea what direction would lead to Octoberskya and the employment agent's office. The courage that had taken her so far from home evaporated. She was not her sister, brave and smart. No, she was a foolish schoolgirl. If she could not get across Moscow, how had she ever imagined she would make it to America? Although she had promised herself she wouldn't cry, one small tear escaped her eye and ran down her cheek.

"What could be so bad, to make a pretty girl like you cry?" The boy was maybe sixteen, tall and skinny. His hair was spiked up in punky points. He had on Levi's and a Megadeth tee shirt.

"Soot in my eye, from the train, it's nothing." He was cute, but Nika had been warned about boys and what they want, especially Moscow boys. Hard currency boys. They made their money trading anything from cigarettes to computers to drugs.

"Let me look." He took a bandanna from his back pocket and stepped close to her.

"It's fine now, really, I'm fine." Nika gave him her surest smile, but a small quiver at the corner of her mouth gave her away.

"I wouldn't dream of hurting you," the boy said, "you look lost, that's all. First time I came to Moscow I nearly pissed my pants."

"Really?" This time Nika's smile was genuine.

"On my mother's grave," he swore, raising his right hand as if taking an oath. "Have you eaten?"

"Lunch," she admitted.

"You like pizza?"

"I've never had it."

"Then you are in for a treat." He started to walk down the stairs, "Come on, you're not going to turn down pizza, are you?" Fighting years of warnings she followed the boy down into the underground.

Shakey's was a US/Russian joint venture. It only accepted hard currency, so it mostly catered to homesick foreigners and black market boys. A large deluxe pie cost slightly less than most Muscovites made in a week.

"Edgar Ivanovich, but everyone calls me Easy E, like the

rapper," the boy said. Nika pulled a slice from her mouth; a long string of cheese stretched to her lips.

"Are you sure I shouldn't use a knife and fork?"

"No, you don't want to look like a country girl, do you?" Through the window, Nika saw a small dark man in an expensive suit staring at her. He had a fine beaver fedora and a walking stick with a gold handle. "Stay away from him. He's a pimp, out trolling for new flesh to peddle."

"No," Nika snapped her eyes from the window, "he can't be, really?"

"He is, trust me."

"You know him?"

"No, but they all look the same, you learn to spot one if you want to survive Moscow."

"I won't be staying here long, I'm going to America," Nika said with finality.

With her stomach full, the exhaustion of the day took hold. It was still hours before the business would be open. Edgar offered to let her sleep at his place.

"I don't know..."

"This town, the mongrels all come out at night, it's not safe for a beautiful girl like you."

"You think I'm beautiful?" She blushed slightly.

"Of course, now come on before I change my mind and leave you here."

His place, as he called it, was in an abandoned warehouse. From scrounged building supplies, he and a group of squatters built a rabbit warren of small rooms. Some had wood doors and walls, others were made of cardboard and tape. Kids and teenagers were piled on every available space. A twelve year old kid in army fatigues sat on the roof of the warehouse, scanning the desolate neighborhood for cops. Not that they had ever been raided. In Moscow, street kids were a disposable nuisance. If no one saw where they went at night, the better for all concerned.

Boys whistled at Edgar and Nika as they moved through the maze of flops. They called her a nice catch and a fine piece of tail. Edgar laughed them off. When he closed the door, sealing them into his small room, Nika felt a building panic. If he tried to hurt her, who would come to her rescue? Certainly none of the street kids she had passed coming in. No, they would probably join in his fun. The room was claustrophobically small. Room enough for a sleeping bag and two rusted folding chairs. A ratty bathroom cabinet was nailed to the wall.

Edgar slid a folding chair over to the door and sat down, blocking her exit. "Lay down, before you fall over."

"Where will you sleep?"

"I won't, I'm the only lock we've got." Leaning back he pressed his weight against the door. The last thing she saw was Edgar smiling before she slipped into sleep.

CHAPTER 3

MEXICO CITY - AUGUST 15TH 4:16 PM

The train is crowded. Flesh pressed against flesh. No one touches me. They can sense I am not one of them. The pimp I killed at the station provided me with cash for the ticket and gold to pawn. I have lost track of how many I have executed. They are faceless. They do not haunt me. An owl never thinks of the life of a mouse. I stare out the window. I clear my mind. I close my eyes. I sleep.

LOS ANGELES - AUGUST 15TH 7:16 PM

Saturday night and I'm bored to tears. I hit the taco truck and get a carnitas burrito. I power on the hot sauce; if I can't drink I can at least get a chili high. I tried calling the club. Doc said he was taking my shifts and no, Manny didn't want to speak to me. Fuck. Piper was pissed off and not returning my calls. I sat on the hood of my car. Eating and remembering.

"Moses, it's me, really." Cass stood in the doorway. Behind her the Pacific roiled and crashed on the beach. It was

Baja. It had been our home for six months.

"Don't, baby girl. No bullshit."

"You want the truth? No bullshit? Really?"

I was sure I didn't. "Yes, the truth."

"You are a drunk. But I can live with that. You are twenty years too old for me. And I can live with that. But this 'baby girl' bullshit I cannot handle. I'm a woman. But you can't see me that way. And I'm screwed up. Sometimes I need to fuck a stranger I met in a bar, just to stop the noise in my head. That look you have right now, says you'll kill the son of a bitch who fucked your woman? That look. Scares me."

"You done?"

"Just about. I love you, Moses. I do. I can't live up to whoever it is you think you need me to be. Can't." Tears rolled slowly down her set face.

"Is it the suit out in the Escalade that you're leaving me for?"

"I'm leaving with him, not for him. I'm leaving because we're about a week shy of hating each other. I'm sorry you wound up with the bad sister."

"I can't stop being me, Cass."

"I know, Mo, and that's the god damn shame of it. You want me to say maybe we'll meet up down the road?"

"I think enough lies have passed between us, let's end this clean." She moved in. She pressed her lips against mine. She left me staring out over the ocean, I didn't need to look to know the wheels crunching on the gravel was the black Escalade

I'd seen in town for the past week. I hoped he was loaded. She deserved a softer life than the past twenty-two years had given her. I tried not to focus on the fact that her departure coincided with our cash reserves running near empty. I stepped out of our house and walked across the burning sand. The pain felt good. The water was cool as it slammed against my jeans. I dove in and swam out away from the beach. I wondered what would happen if I just kept swimming. Far from the shore, I floated on my back and thought about opening my mouth and letting myself fill with water. Be gone. Instead I swam as long and as hard as I could. I finally dragged myself up onto the beach and passed out. It wasn't long after that I moved back to LA. Took up bouncing again. It was as if nothing had changed. But me. And I'm not even sure I changed that much.

I had to get moving. Heading anywhere. We Angelinos don't feel at home unless we are rolling along. I let the Crown Vic drift up over Silver Lake and down into Hollywood. She was a black, harmless looking ex-cop car, but under her hood beat the heart of a road beast. Bored, stroked and blueprinted. Hi pro cams, new top end. She was all go, no show. "Is it getting better?" Bono asked from the car speakers as I cranked U2 up and let their bleak Irish hope take me away.

Hollywood Boulevard was clogged with cruisers, shined up cars with kids hanging out the windows trying for the ever-important hookup. A lowered '67 Impala with candy apple metal flake paint was pulled to the curb. Its driver, a sixteen year old cholo, was sitting on the curb while the cops shined a light in his girl's face and ran his plates. Had I remembered it was Saturday night, I never would have crossed into Hollywood. Too many cops. Too many kids. Too many hormones running wild.

Cruising down Highland, I crossed Melrose into

Hancock Park. Expensive homes sat a coin toss from the homeless of Hollywood. The wind blew my sedan west on Pico. Down past the Mexican restaurants with the new immigrants, still wet from the crossing, eating bowls of goat's head soup. Across Fairfax, where all the signs were suddenly in Hebrew, goys need not apply. Up over the hill and past the tall sound stages of 20th Century Fox, where the gates are heavily guarded to insure that no original ideas sneak onto the lot. Under the 405 freeway and there it was, calling me like a siren to the rocks. Fantasia's neon blinked "Girls Girls Girls" and "Bikini Contest." Even though I'd never been there before, I knew I was home. I could smell the stale beer, cheap perfume, sweat and desperation mixing with the thump of bass-driven dance music, leaking out the back door into the parking lot.

"Five bucks," a skinny Vietnamese valet said, ready for me to argue with him.

"Twenty. I park it, you watch it. Sound fair?" I said shooting him my best I'm-not-going-to-eat-you smile. He must have been a tough guy, because he smiled back, usually people don't.

"Okey doke," he said. I walked towards the club, wondering what the hell I hoped to find here that wasn't back at Club Xtasy, except maybe a job. That would show Manny.

"I saw her standing there." Cheesy Brit pop assaulted my ears as I pushed through the curtains into Fantasia's bikini bar. It must be said, The Beatles were pussies. John, Paul, George and that goofy mutant Ringo, pussies one and all. With their whiny, simpering love songs and simple solutions to complex questions. "Love is all you need." Tell that to an eight year old boy whose mother is a mean drunk Jesus freak who thinks cornflakes are dinner. Fuck love, what I needed when she took a belt to my ass was a .44 and an airtight alibi.

I dropped a ten on the counter girl and looked around the big dark hall of a room. Citizens were lined up three deep at the bar. On stage, a chick in a day glow orange string bikini was twisting the night away for a group of Asian businessmen. Kneeling down, she let them stuff singles into her bikini top and cop a quick feel of her silicone-stuffed tits.

"Manager around tonight?"

"Every night, you a bouncer?"

"What, my size gave me away?"

"No, you just don't dress hip enough to be a DJ, and you sure ain't no dancer."

"Could be a bartender."

"Don't have the style to pull that off either. No, bouncer it is."

"Fine. Point me towards his office."

She smirked and flicked a thumb over her shoulder. I pushed through the crowd, smiling at all the lovelies. Damn, a fine woman can bring a smile to my face.

When I knocked at the office door a smokey woman's voice told me to enter.

She sat behind the desk, all three hundred and fifty pounds of her.

"You a bouncer?"

"Yeah."

"Where did you work?"

"Xtasy."

"I know Manny, how did you fuck him?"

"Didn't. Caught a girl freelancing. Stopped it. Some teeth may have gotten broken, maybe a rib or two."

She let out a fleshy rumbling laugh. "What part of Eastern Europe did the girl come from?"

"How did you know where she was from?"

"Just a guess."

"Any chance of picking up a shift?"

"Not a chance in hell. I don't want to go to war with that Persian bastard Manny over a bouncer. We understand?"

"Sure, I'll get out of your way."

"Look, tell you what I'll do - leave me your number, I'll call Manny, if he's cool, maybe something could be worked out. Could use a big no-shit guy like you.

I left her office with the promise of a call and a free drink pass. I stood by the bar, planning not to drink. Letting my eyes move over the back bar until I spotted it: McCallans. But no, I was not going to drink.

"You want a drink?"

"Yes." I answered without hesitation.

"McCallans, right? You're staring at it with intent."

"Really?"

"And now you're staring at my tits." She was a Japanese

24

girl with cropped platinum hair. "So which will it be, tits or scotch?"

"Let's start with scotch and see where that leads us."

It's called a slip, like you hit some black ice and booze fell into your mouth. Bullshit. Watching that magical amber liquid fill the glass I felt like I was coming home from a long lonely trip. I lifted the glass. First the smell, like liquid peat smoke. Then the taste, clean. Then the warmth.

"Again."

"You and that glass want to get a room?" She was grinning playfully at me as she filled my glass and moved down the bar. The second drink I sipped. In the mirror behind the bar I could scan the colorful dancing room. I felt the tension and rage drift away.

I caught a glimpse of a brassy red haired girl. Spun around and near toppled a burly man in a paint-streaked work shirt. He pivoted, fast, ready, his fist cocked down low. He met my eyes.

"Whoa, Cowboy," I said, eyes going flat. "This ain't the OK Corral, and I'm not the black hat."

"That's racially insensitive," he said, not relaxing a muscle.

"What?"

"Black hat. It implies and supports the racist view that black is bad and by contrast, white is good."

"I'm not a racist."

"I'm sure Hitler and his gang of psychopathic fuck-heads

said the same. Point is, racists never say they're racist."

"That's it, motherfucker, first you call me a racist, now a Nazi. Why don't we take a little stroll outside so I can kick your..." My words were cut short by a thick black man pressed into overalls and a net shirt.

"We got a problem, Earl?" he said to the man.

"No problem, I was simply schooling this man in the inherent racism of modern English."

The big man shook his head, looking at me with a knowing sadness. "Call you a racist?"

"And a Nazi."

"You're not the first to want to pummel him. Earl, you be a madman!"

"Thank you, sir." Earl's eyes flicking between us.

"But he's our madman." He dropped enough edge into his voice to make it clear Earl was under his protection.

"I get it." I jutted out a hand to this fellow bouncer. "Name's Moses McGuire."

"They call me Mac." He smiled, showing me several gold teeth.

"As in 'truck'?"

"To the guys 'round here."

"And 'Daddy' to the ladies?"

"Pow, give the man a toy doll." With a wink, he floated off to look for real trouble. I settled in for a drink with my new friend, local artist and cunning linguist, Earl. The club was a bikini bar, so the girls stripped down to bra and panties. Most of the action took place in the VIP room. The lack of nudity gave the place the feeling of the prom these guys never had. Only at this prom, their dates were wearing outfits from Victoria's Secret and if the floor man wasn't looking, they could get nasty in the back room.

Antony and the Johnsons filling the room with their sad operatic heartbreaking sound. Earl was droning on about the power of the Industrial Arts Movement or some such crap I didn't understand when I saw her...

On stage, a backlit silhouette, tall, lithe, with the muscular body of a ballet dancer. She rose up on the balls of her feet and started to spin, extending her arms as she did. The front lights came up, shining off her long chestnut hair. A lump caught in my throat. I spent my nights surrounded by pretty girls, but she took my breath away. She had a delicate face with strong high cheek bones. Her full lips were slightly parted, showing the small gap in her front teeth. This small imperfection only made her more beautiful. But what really nailed me were her eyes, sea green, they sparkled in the lights. It was as if she was holding some wonderful secret behind those eyes. She looked twenty-five, but I bet she was younger.

"Last of the true aristocrats, a Romanoff I'm sure." Earl's voice came from far off.

"What?"

"Our Katerina. She escaped the Bolsheviks, crossed the frozen..." I stopped listening when her glittering eyes singled me out of the crowd and locked in like a sniper's laser. She held the pole, swaying slowly to the half beat of Antony and the Johnsons. Slow and seductive, she was desire incarnate. Those eyes calling me to her. Telling me all this was mine, it always had been, it always would be.

Never breaking our eye contact, I walked past the tables of drunks and dancers toward the stage. I dropped two twenties at her feet. She came to the edge of the stage and leaned down, whispering "thank you" in my ear. She had a thick accent, and the feel of her warm breath sent tingles up my back. Grabbing the pole, she flipped up so she was suspended in the air by her thighs. Arching her back she hung with her arms extended, tilting back her head, she gave me a wicked smile.

The song ended, guys clapped, a few threw money. She was good, she hadn't even taken her clothes off and I was breaking a sweat. It was as if she had been dancing only for me, I knew it was an act, but it felt real. She was that good.

"Smitten, are we?" Earl said, as I knocked back another scotch.

"No, just appreciate talent when I see it."

"She's from Moscow... Oh my god! How do I look?" he almost shouted. He had seen something over my shoulder.

"I don't swing that way, not that I'm not flattered."

"Be serious. Is my hair ok, it's not flipping up? Oh damn. Damn..." He was about to have an aneurysm.

"You look fine, Earl."

"Really? You're not just saying that?"

"No, really. You look good," I said, knowing it wouldn't matter how he looked. He bounced across the room to a cute little thing in a Catholic schoolgirl's skirt and spikes, who smiled and hugged him. She was half his age. She had high end store bought tits. Leading him to a booth she crawled in beside him laughing at something he said. Before this night was over he'd be down a bill or two and feeling good about himself, because some pretty young thing was attracted to him. If it worked for him, it was cheaper and more effective than a shrink.

The whiskey was taking effect. The room swirled pleasantly. I had reached that wonderful level of tipsy, the place where trouble goes away, judgment is skewed but not gone. I watched Earl and his schoolgirl cuddle, I was happy for him.

"You like young girl better?" I spun around to find Katerina standing next to me.

"No. Watching a friend fall in love."

"A fool's game, yes?" She looked over at Earl and smiled. "And that man is a fool. Last week, he brought her roses."

"He's alright, he's just a little too smart to figure out how it works here."

"And you?" Her voice was deep with a sexy nicotine rasp. Sliding onto the stool next to me she searched my eyes.

"I gave you the only roses that matter." I rubbed my thumb and fingers together in the universal sign for cash. "And I don't expect any return, except the fun of watching you strut that stage."

"Buy me drink?" she said, absentmindedly tracing her finger down the line of her dress, pulling my attention to her breasts. They were mounded by a push-up bra into marvelously lush cleavage.

"Nice move," I said, my eyes following her finger, "but unnecessary. I already noticed how good you look."

"I don't know what you are talking about," she went wide-eyed and innocent.

"You're hot, you know it. I know it. I'm way out of my league here, so I'll buy you a drink, chit some chat while you scope your next victim, but you have to turn down the heat, ok?"

"Spasibo, it was much work, pretending to like a big handsome man like you." She smiled broadly, showing me that gap in her teeth. "Betty, please, a Rémy," she called to the bartender.

She had expensive taste when someone else was paying. I wondered what she drank when it went on her tab. I ordered myself another McCallans that I probably didn't need, but sure wanted.

"Na zdororve!" she said, clinking my shot glass with her snifter. I knew she got a cut of any booze the chumps bought her, but I didn't care. It was worth every penny to sit listening to her accented broken English.

"Scorpio, yes?" she asked.

"I don't know."

"What is you birthday?"

"October twentieth. What? Why are you grinning like I just dropped a hundred on the stage?"

"Scorpio. Casanova, Scorpio the lover. Ruled by Mars, a lover and warrior."

"And you?" Astrology is pure mumbo jumbo, but I would have said anything to keep the conversation going.

"Me, Aries. We are fire and water."

"Is that a good thing?"

"Yes." She slew me with a look of deep longing. "My beautiful man, I knew you were for me, first time I saw you," she said, simply as if it were an obvious fact.

"I thought we agreed you were going to dial it back," I said, hoping she would turn up the heat.

"Scorpio," she shook her head, mulling the thought over, "I have to be very careful with you, if I fall for you it would be very bad for business."

"Why me? Look around, plenty of younger, richer guys here."

"They are boys dressed like men. You are man."

"Dressed like a boy." I smiled looking down at my Pogues concert shirt, faded jeans and Doc Martens.

I spent my nights looking after girls, but here was a woman. My back straightened and my chest puffed slightly. She made me want to be the man she seemed to think I was.

Katy Perry blasted happy pop over the sound system. I noticed Earl and his schoolgirl had disappeared into the VIP room, so I guessed his date was going fine. Over our drinks, Katerina told me she was from Yaroslavl, a small city two hundred miles from Moscow. "When I was fifteen, my mother passed away and left me to take care of my baby sister and my pig of a father."

"Sounds rough." I never knew my old man and by the time I was sixteen I was in the Marines being shot at by towelheads in the Root. To get away from my drunk mother, I had stolen my big brother's birth certificate and they shipped me off to that jug fuck in Lebanon. I didn't tell Katerina any of that, I just told her I had grown up poor, too. We had a bond that children forced to grow up too soon share. A bond of pain and longing. A bond of anger and the desire to be loved. Over our words, a separate conversation flowed between our eyes, a conversation of longing and need.

"Come, I'll dance for you. I want to."

"Sorry, I don't do that anymore," I said, with zero resolve.

"Yes, I know... come." She took my hand and led me willingly across the room and through the red velvet curtains into the VIP room. Earl must have gone home while we were talking, because we had the room to ourselves. It was a low-ceilinged dimly lit cave of lust. Plush crushed velvet tuck and roll surrounded the room like it was one big low-rider Chevy. There were several tables with chairs and candles. Generally the couch is $35-$40 bucks and the chairs are $20-$25. That's before tip, but only about half the pricks tip the girl who dances on them. The law states that the man cannot at any time touch the girl, she can touch him, but not in a lewd manner. Trying to legislate morality is like trying to hold back the sea with a chain-link fence.

Katerina pushed me down in the soft padding, over the speakers, Cee Lo Green started singing about wishing he had enough cash to keep the girl. She put her knees between mine and pried them open, moving slowly ever closer. I was used to lap grind, make a guy come and get on with your day dances. But she was seducing me, one move at a time. As she swayed closer, I could feel the heat emanating from her before any skin touched. Her lips brushed across my cheek, I could feel her breath, smell the faint cigarette mixed with brandy. Just when I thought she would kiss me she pulled back. It took all I had not to pull her down on top of me. The song ended and Katerina rose up taking a small step back. Her eyes flicked down to my lap.

"One more, yes?" she said.

"Why not." I fought to sound like I could take it or leave it. Chili Peppers' *Breaking the Girl* filled the air around us. Katerina slowly unfastened her shirt, letting it drop to the floor. She stepped out of her leather skirt and stood for a moment so I could look at her. She had a ragged appendix scar. A small jail-blue tattoo started on her hip and ran down disappearing into her thong. It was maybe two inches long, a straight line with a cross bar near the top and below it a second line set more diagonally. Marina had a similar tat, it must be a Russian thing.

Looking up at Katerina, I knew whatever she wanted was hers, she was that beautiful. Sounds shallow but there it is. Moving between my legs, this time she pushed her leg until it was against my erection. I let out a shudder as she began to stroke me with her thigh. Moving up she brushed her breasts across my face, I kissed her ivory skin. She didn't pull away. She moved slowly down, I kissed her neck, and then she brought me her lips. Gift of all gifts, a real kiss. Hookers and strippers alike will tell you they will fuck and suck all day long, but to kiss is just too personal.

Katerina's lips pressed against mine. She bit at my lower lip, her eyes were closed and her breathing had the rhythm of arousal. Her hand wrapped around the line in my jeans, she let out a small gasp. I ran my hand up her thigh. Continuing the kiss, I pulled her down on top of me. And like two Catholic teenagers, we went at. She ground herself against my bulge, pushing her tongue into my mouth. How many songs came and went while we pounded against each other I haven't a clue, I was lost in the rush. Her breathing turned into a deep rasp. Suddenly her eyes popped open in crazy surprise. She sank her teeth into my shoulder to muffle her scream. Then like a rag doll, she collapsed into the couch next to me with her head on my shoulder.

"Oh, oh... you didn't finish... I sorry... I," she said with weak but genuine concern.

"Ain't nothin but a thing."

"But..."

"Hush... you smell so human." I nuzzled her neck.

"What?"

"You don't cover up with a bunch of perfume, you smell human."

Her eyes drifted closed, maybe she wanted to block out the room around us.

"What's your name? It's not 'Katerina'."

"You don't like it?"

"It's fine, just not yours, least not the one you were born with."

She thought about this for a long moment, screwing up her fine features. "What is your name?"

"Moses McGuire."

"That's funny."

"The only book my mother ever read was the bible. Brother's name is 'Luke'. Guess we're both lucky we didn't get stuck with 'Jesus One' and 'Jesus Two'."

She opened her eyes, making sure I knew what she was giving me. "Anya Kolpacolva."

Somewhere out in the club, the DJ was calling for all the girls to line up for a two for the price of one lap dance special. Anya let out a laugh. "Oh my god, how long have we been here? You are bad for business, I know this the moment I see you."

"Do you mind?"

"No," she said laughing. Jumping up, she pulled on her shirt and skirt in faster time than an Indy pit crew. Reaching down, she tugged me up and out of the couch. Arm in arm and giggling like high schoolers, we walked out of the VIP room. When I slipped $200 into her purse she rolled her eyes but she didn't refuse. She had rent to pay like everyone else.

From the bar, I watched the money mating dance gyrate around me. Anya slipped like a shark through the sea of men, hustling them, then stopping by to give me a wink or a kiss in between trips to the VIP room. I realized one of these fat fucks was gonna wind up dead if I didn't get out of there soon.

"Want a dance?" Anya had slipped up behind me while my concentration was on buying a last shot of scotch.

"Love to, but I'm broke." I don't know why I lied, fact was I had a wad in my pocket and more cash stashed in my hideout hole in the car. I guess I was hoping she would offer me a freebee, a way she could show that I was different than the other slobs.

"We have ready-teller." She made it sound sexy, purring like it was some exotic love toy.

"Do I look like the kind of guy they'd give a bank card to?"

"Everyone has bank card."

"I don't."

"Too bad," she was leaning into me, making sure I got a grand glimpse down her dress at what I was missing. She kissed my neck. "You are so bad for business."

"When do you get off? I'll take you to breakfast," I whispered.

"A date?" She closed her eyes, smiling inwardly at the idea. "No, not tonight." Past my shoulder, she surveyed the room for her next client.

"Whatever." I turned back to the bar, trying to pull off indifference, though petulant may have been closer to the effect.

"Here." She was on the move, she slipped a piece of paper into my hand. "My cell number, call me." She started to disappear into the crowd, then turned back. "You do have a cell phone?"

"Nope, but I've got some change and a working finger."

"My beautiful man. Are you sure you are American?"

"Only because my parents fucked here," I said. Anya laughed, running her hand through my hair. I gave her a stolen kiss the manager didn't see and promised to come back the next night. Then stumbled out into the evening.

CHAPTER 4

The Vietnamese car park was sleeping in a chair leaned against the building. I climbed behind the wheel of the beast, but lacked the will to make my hand turn the ignition. What kind of candy-ass falls for a dancer's bullshit?

I held the napkin with her number on it, like somehow it proved she wanted me for more than the money in my wallet. I knew, had clear evidence that it would all end bad for me. But here I was, sitting in my car, hoping we would ride off into the sunrise together.

I had watched the slobs at the club and puffed myself full of superiority. This was a job for these girls and the men were the work the girls had to do to knock out their bills. And here I was, sitting behind the wheel hoping to catch a glimpse of Anya when she came out.

Every promise I'd made myself, no more drinking, no more lap dances, had been shot to shit in one night. The new and improved me would have to take a rain check.

At one forty-five, the drunks and dandies left the club in one long stream. The younger men who had come with buddies joked and whooped at each other. The older men moved with heads down, hoping to hide their secret shame. Within minutes, the lot was almost empty.

At two ten, Anya and a short red-haired dancer walked out of the club. Anya was dressed in jeans and a hooded sweat-shirt. Street clothes only made her look better, more real. I was about to get out and call to her when a black Mercedes pulled to the curb. The redhead opened the door and they climbed into the back.

On the Westside, Mercedes are more common than skin cancer. But this was the second time I had seen Russian dancers get into a black S class. I couldn't swear it was the same one that had picked up Marina, but what were the odds?

Maybe I saw a mobster where there was a car service, but I didn't think so.

For a moment, I tried to convince myself that it was none of my business who they were or how Anya was involved. But when the Mercedes pulled off, I followed. Slipping into traffic a few cars back, I gave them just enough room to roam without noticing me.

The difference between stalking and looking after someone is a fine line, one I decided not to look too closely at as I followed them up Wilshire. At Santa Monica Boulevard they hung a left heading past Beverly Hills, towards Little Kiev, West Hollywood's Russian neighborhood. Cruising up to an intersection, they slowed down, timing it right so they could blast across the street at the moment the light turned red.

The cars in front of me stopped, blocking me in. I

angled into the right-hand turning lane and mashed down the gas pedal. The V8 roared its deep throated war cry as I blasted through the red. I swerved to avoid an oncoming 4x4. They fisted their horn, but I was gone in a cloud of burning rubber.

Two blocks up, I saw the Mercedes squealing left down a small side street. My heart thumped to an adrenaline-driven beat. I wished I hadn't left my piece at home. With two felony convictions on my back, I never carried unless I was expecting trouble. The three strikes bullshit meant that a firearms bust would buy me the bitch.

I lost sight of the Mercedes when they ripped a quick left down a narrow alley that ran behind a two-story office building. Pulling down the alley, I discovered it was blocked off at the other end by a cement block wall. The Mercedes had vanished. Rolling to a stop halfway to the wall, I searched for their escape route.

Headlights shot into the sky. The Mercedes sped up out of a parking ramp behind me and skidded to a stop sideways, blocking my exit. I was trapped, and whatever came next, I knew it wasn't going to be good. If I was right and they were Russian mob, it was going to get ugly.

The front passenger door opened and the biggest man I've ever seen lumbered out. I'm a big man. This guy was a fucking giant. A freak. He had a huge square head, with a tattooed line of barbed wire running across his forehead. His black beard and thick hair were buzzed to military length. He was wearing a loose black suit with a black tee shirt stretched tight across his massive chest muscles. He walked slowly toward my car. I could clearly make out the bulge of a shoulder holster under his designer jacket.

I jumped out of the Crown Vic, and headed for the

brute at a run. Calm in his sizable advantage, he noticed too late that I brought a tire iron behind my back. Only losers bitch about a fair fight. I arced the iron up toward his head. It would have been a great move if he hadn't raised his arm and taken the blow on his forearm. The tire iron landed with a meaty thud. If it hurt, he didn't show it on his face.

Fuck. This man was a fucking monster. Swinging back to strike again, I never got the chance. He drove a boulder sized fist into my chest, exploding the air out of my lungs and sending me stumbling back. In battle, the whole world slows to a syrupy crawl. I was fighting for breath when I saw his other fist sailing at me. I had time to notice four skulls tattooed on his knuckles before it connected under my jaw. My head snapped back and my feet left the ground, for a floating moment I thought everything was going to be fine. It wasn't. I crashed down hard. Lightning sparks darted across my vision and my stomach lurched.

In the back of the Mercedes, Anya had her face pressed to the glass. She looked worried, and in a sick way I was glad. As if it were a sign she liked me. A boot to my ribs made me forget her.

The brute towered over me like King Kong on steroids. I was blurry-eyed and gasping, he hadn't even broken a sweat. I fought to get up, but he placed one of his size 15s on my chest and vised me to the ground.

"Kak dela mudack?" a voice said from behind the giant. My chest was compressed to the point where it took all my strength to keep breathing; speaking was way beyond my power.

"You want Pasha to squash you?" The driver moved out of the giant's shadow. He was a thin angular Russian, his head was clean-shaven and he had a bushy black Stalin mustache. A prison tattoo of a cat crawled up out of his open shirt collar, scratching its way onto his cheek. On his knuckles I saw two tattooed skulls.

"Who are you?" he asked.

Only a gasp passed my lips. My head was throbbing and I could feel the flush of blood pulsing in my face.

"Vzdrochennyi," the giant said with a low chuckle.

"Da." The driver pointed a bony finger at my face. "Pasha says, you look like cock that's been jerked too hard." The brick-like foot on my chest twisted, grinding out what was left of my breath. "You fucked up his jacket, is it your destiny to die under his boot?" I struggled out a head shake. "Ok, maybe it is, maybe it isn't. We'll see. Pasha?" He motioned up and the giant stepped off me. Air flooded in, burning my starved lungs. "Now, who the fuck are you, dolboy'eb? Why follow me?"

"I wasn't," I mumbled out as best as I could. A flick from the driver's eyes and the giant's huge hands ripped through my pockets. Rolling me over, he pulled my wallet out of my jeans. It had cash only no ID, I never carried any. It's easier to be whoever you want when you carry no evidence to the contrary.

"Victor!" The redhead called from the back seat of the car. The thin man walked over and spoke Russian into the window. She said something that made Anya shake her head in denial. Her eyes flicked briefly onto me, then back to the man.

"The girl tells me you were dancing with Anya. Says you were talking a long time. No badge, no gun, not a cop. Who are you?"

"I work... for Mr. Gallico." Trying to regain some level of calm, I rolled up into a sitting position. I fought the urge to massage my bruised jaw. Dropping LA's mob boss' name wasn't a total bluff, I'd known the old Sicilian since I was a kid. I didn't work for him, but he owed me a few favors.

"Fuck the guinea bastard," the driver said. "What is he to me?"

"He's the man who's going to have your eggs scrambled if you don't watch out." I was making it up as fast as my thumping head could think. These bastards could kill me and never look back. My only hope was to convince them that killing me might piss off their boss.

"Why would the Italians have you follow me?" He wasn't convinced yet, but doubt was starting to show.

"Word is, you're running whores in Hollywood. That's his territory, and you ignorant pricks know it." I knew I was pushing it, but if the bluff was going to work, I needed to act like I had the upper hand.

"The wop bastard, he controls shit," he said without conviction.

"Then kill me and let it fall where it does." I gave him the hardest stare I could muster.

"Maybe you bullshit."

"Yeah, and maybe I'm not. Want to risk a war with the Italians to find out?"

"Pososi moyu konfetku." He backhanded me across the face, but after the giant's blow it felt like a love tap. "I see you in my rearview mirror again, you will be dead."

"Don't worry, if I come up behind you again, you won't notice me until the blood's running down your cheap suit."

"Cheap? Versace!" He looked like he was going to smack me again. My cold eyes caught him off balance. If he was going to kill me, so be it. I was tired of playing the bitch to his macho gangster act.

With a twitch of his head he led the giant back to the Mercedes. It would have been comical watching the massive man fold himself into the car if my head wasn't hurting so bad. In the red glow of their brake lights, I saw Anya through the rear window. She looked both frightened and sadly resigned.

While they faded into dark streets, I stayed sitting. Feeling for broken bones, I was relieved to find only bruises and scrapes. The first thing you learn in the military is keep your head down and never volunteer for anything. Only a cherry would go rushing off to try and save a woman he'd just met from a fate she may or may not have chosen. If I could have erased her scared eyes from my mind, I would have. And if my mother had three wheels, she would have been a trike. Besides, take Anya out of the picture, I still owed the Russian bastards. You let someone take you down without retribution you've started down that soapy path that ends with you being their shower toy.

The combination of whisky and pain made my drive home a real bundle of joy. I lived in a small rented house in Highland Park, a Latin neighborhood in northeast LA. The yuppies tired of housing prices in Silver Lake and the Westside had started moving into the adjoining areas. We could hear the drums of urban renewal beating, but for now our corner of LA was safe.

Coming through my door, I was knocked down by hundred and twenty-two pounds of hurling Bullmastiff. Her name was Angel and she had been my dog since her owner was killed. She was my first pet. I always thought it was hard enough to take care of myself, why would I want an animal? But the fact was, she had squirmed her way into my heart. It was good to have a warm body to come home to.

Downing five aspirins with a tall glass of water, I crawled into bed. With a snap of my finger, Angel jumped onto the bed and curled up beside me. We were both snoring moments after I shut off the light.

CHAPTER 5

MEXICO CITY - AUGUST 16TH 5:23 AM

Nika looked down on Mexico City as the plane circled for a landing. Volcanoes rose up above the brown haze that smothered the sprawling metropolis. It had been over twenty-four hours since she left Moscow. In Tel Aviv, she met a man in a very nice suit who had taken her Russian passport and given her an Israeli one. The picture the agent in Moscow had taken was on the new passport, but the name was not hers. When the man in the nice suit gave her a ticket and led her to the gate, he warned her not to talk to anyone until she was met in Mexico. With a kiss on each cheek he sent her off onto the plane. The last real sleep she had gotten was in Edgar's squat. She stayed with him for three days while the arrangements were made for her trip. The only time he tried to kiss her was just before she climbed into the employment agent's car to leave, and that was a sweet chaste kiss. She couldn't believe how suspicious she had been of Edgar. He was nice, and sitting alone on the plane she wished he had come with her. This was her first trip in an airplane. She tried to sleep, but every bump of turbulence sent her heart into a rapid tattoo.

Nika let out an involuntary gasp when the wheels hit the runway. Many of the other passengers applauded the landing. Taxiing to the gate, they sat for several minutes with the seat-belt light still lit. Around her, people ignored the voice on the intercom advising them to please remain seated. The door slid open and a uniformed Mexican official walked onto the plane, followed by a young soldier. Passengers cleared the aisles and let him pass. In his hand he held a form and was checking it against the seat numbers. He stopped when he got to Nika's row, looking her over carefully. Nika knew it was too good to be true. Somehow they had found out her plans. Now she would be sent back to Russia. She had been crazy to imagine she could escape her fate. The official checked his form once more and then spoke to her. She didn't understand a word he spoke, but when he motioned for her to follow him, she understood. She walked with her head down, eyes averted from the other passengers, ashamed that so many had witnessed her failure.

With the official in front and the soldier behind, they led her past the customs lines and through a door into a small office. The official sat behind a desk and motioned for Nika to take a seat across from him. He spoke in racing Spanish, and only when he saw her lost eyes did he switch to English. "Do you speak English?"

"Yes." Nika was relieved they had a common language.

"Passport please." Nika handed it over and watched as he stamped it and stapled a form to it. "This is your student visa, it will allow you to stay in Mexico until you travel norte." Placing her passport into an envelope, he handed it to the soldier, who stood at attention behind Nika. "Welcome to Mexico, and good luck on your travels."

"Thank you." Nika couldn't believe what was happening, she could barely keep herself from shrieking with joy. The soldier led her through a series of halls that traversed the airport out of the public eye. They came out onto a freight dock where a white van was waiting. A middle-aged man with a face ruined by acne scars took the envelope from the soldier and opened the back of the van, it was windowless, like a dark cave. The man pointed for Nika to get in. Something about the man and the van scared her, but she pulled up her courage, reminding herself that nothing good ever came easily. Crawling into the van, she found no seats, only stained rough woven blankets and a few dirty pillows. The slamming door almost caught her feet as she scrambled to get in.

As her eyes adjusted to the dark, she discovered she was not alone. Pressed up against the far wall, two eyes gleamed.

LOS ANGELES - AUGUST 16TH 7:16 AM

A huge sloppy dog kiss woke me. Angel could sleep through the end of the world, but miss breakfast by ten minutes and she broke out in a rash. I had a sick gut and a head full of regret. I felt slow and clogged from my return to drinking. My mouth was dry, swollen and tasted like gym socks. That was it I told myself, no more drinking, I was done, time to climb back up on the wagon.

I poured two cups of kibble into a bowl for Angel and lumbered into the shower. While the hot water worked on my kinked muscles, I tried to reconstruct the previous night. Anya flitting across my inner-vision, beautiful and scared. The Russians picked up Marina at my club, then later Anya and the redhead in Santa Monica. The smaller of the two thugs, the one called Victor, had as much as admitted they were running whores when he denied that they did it in Hollywood. Was the blow job in my parking lot a one-time deal as Marina told me, or was she hooking out of the club and giving the cash to Victor? Was that the new scam, place girls in strip clubs so they could troll for Johns? Why not place an ad on Craigslist?

All these questions but no solid answers. It was time to reach out to Anya and find out what the fuck was going on. Drying off, I discovered a goose egg on the back of my skull, and a dark bruise had flowered on my jaw. Gifts from Victor and the giant.

"Privet! Smart boy, you found me, but sadly I am busy. You know what to do, so do it." At the beep, I hung up without leaving a number. I didn't know if Anya's calls were being monitored. I made the call from a pay phone, if they checked her missed calls it wouldn't give me up. The less they knew about me the better.

"Walk away, boss. You don't want to fuck with these psycho Russians," Gregor said as we sat the next morning, drinking thick Turkish coffee in his Frogtown apartment. "The ink - barbed wire across his head - that's gulag shit. He was down for life without parole. The skulls, they get one for every man they murder."

"Maybe they were fronting. Half the punks with spider webs never been locked down or even heard of the Aryan Brotherhood," I said.

"No. Russian cons will kill anyone with ink he didn't earn. First they cut the offending skin off. Sweet, yeah?" Gregor was a young Armenian thug, a big boy, six foot and pushing 250 hard. A blanket of baby fat surrounded his face, but the rest was pure muscle. When I met him, I'd broken his nose, then I'd hired him to cover my ass in a rescue mission that went sideways. He took a blast from an AK47 that ripped him up and left scars from his chest to his left knee. He never complained. After he recuperated, I set him up with an apartment outside of the grip of the Glendale Armenian Power boys. I had Manny hire him as a day bouncer. Plenty will say they got your back, Gregor had proven it. In our world, that was better than gold.

"Anya, the dancer, she had a tattoo on her hip, like a telephone pole."

"Same as Marina?"

"Exactly."

"Not a telephone pole, it's a Russian cross. You'd know that if you weren't a heathen."

"Fine, church boy, so what's it mean?"

"Old country bullshit. The Vors would mark the girls in their stable. A warning to other pimps to keep them from poaching."

"Fuck me."

"Yup, and they will. These guys are ruthless in ways you can't even imagine. Best plan, forget the girlie."

"Not an option."

"Always an option. Put one foot in front of the other 'til this is a bad memory. Or is she that fine?"

"She is, if she's real. If she's playing me, I'm fucked."

"Either way you're fucked, boss. You want me to ride

along?"

"Unless you got something better to do."

"Nothing that can't wait."

At nine PM, I loaded my Smith & Wesson snub nosed .38 and dropped it into the pocket of my black leather sports coat. I slipped a Buck knife into my Levi's then laced up my steel-toed Docs. If the shit went sideways, I was going to be ready this time. I picked up Gregor; no bulge showed under his wool greatcoat, but I knew he had his CZ 9mm strapped up under his arm.

Hitting the freeway, I cranked up Amanda Palmer, piano, accordion, hell, even ukulele, all in a punk sound - it was as if the decadent Germany of the twenties had been brought back and replayed through a busted speaker. It was one of the few CDs Gregor and I could agree on. Left alone, I would have played The Clash's *Give 'Em Enough Rope*. Bar none, the single best record ever made. Perfect for the necessary mind-set I was looking for, fuck 'em all and let god sort it out. Someday, I would convince Gregor of the importance of The Clash, but it didn't seem like this was the time. Settling into a groove on the freeway, I concentrated on the music. Trick was to let the sound take my head off the present situation. When you have no facts, it's best not to let your mind make shit up. Conjecture killed more good men than bad intel.

I parked down a side street around the corner from Fantasia's. Moving in the shadows, I scanned for the marauding Mercedes Benz. I couldn't see Gregor but I knew he was somewhere on the street with his eyes on me.

"Anya called in sick, said she was visited by the monthly red tide," Mac told me as we leaned against the bar. "Lot of that going around on Sunday nights. Slow as frozen molasses."

"Got an address on her?"

"No, wouldn't give it up if I did."

"Fair enough.   Her friend, the Russian redhead, she come in tonight?"

"Tatyana?   Sure, she's in the lap room.   You wanna dance, just wait 'til her man of the moment is broke."

I waited for the time it took to drink two cokes.   I turned down several offers to have my world rocked by the bored dancers.   Finally, the curtains parted and Tatyana led a rumpled looking older gentleman out.   She was a zoftig little girl, maybe five feet five and that was in heels, she had copper-penny colored hair cut in a short bob.   They had only taken a few steps before I was at her side.

"Sorry, pal, I'm on a dinner break, you'll understand I'm in a hurry," I said, taking her hand.

"Sure, um, alright, I guess," he stammered.

She followed me into the VIP room.   I snapped the curtain closed behind us.

"You want a dance?   Or maybe something more pleasing?"   Her voice was a practiced combination of raw lust and innocence.   Her accent was thick, but designed to be charming and exotic.   Sitting down on one of the sofas, she looked up at me, wide eyed.

"Where's Anya?"   I stood over her.

"Who?" She looked at my bruised jaw. "I know you."

"Let's cut through the bullshit, I saw you in the car with Anya. Where is she?"

"Victor's going to kill you."

"He your pimp?"

"He's our driver. Keeps us safe from crazy Americans who don't know a fuck is a fuck, not a love affair." Her young eyes had turned cold and jaded. "Now you want a dance or a blow job or a fuck? No? I go back to work."

She started to stand. Placing a hand on her shoulder, I held her in place. My free hand snatched her purse off the sofa. "I'll scream," she said unconvincingly.

"And I'll clue Mac in on your side action... Your choice."

"You have no idea who you are fucking with."

"That's right, I don't."

"They can reach out and flick, your life is over, no one can stop them. You are a walking corpse, but you don't know it." Her eyes were beady and lifeless.

"If I believed every person who told me I was dead, I wouldn't have made it out of the fifth grade." She shrugged and studied her fingernails with practiced indifference. I rifled through her bag and came up with a cell phone, a wad of bills, a counterfeit driver's license with an address in Brentwood and a postcard from Moscow. The note on the back was all squiggles, backward letters and too many consonants to make sense, but the address was in English. It was in West Hollywood's Little Kiev, not far from where Victor and the giant had braced me.

"All I'm going to do is make sure Anya's ok. If she's copacetic, I'm gone and you're free to continue business as usual. But if you get stupid and call Victor, folks are going to die." I dropped a fifty and walked out, hoping she was smart or scared enough to keep her mouth shut.

"This goes down twisted, we could wind up in a lake," I said.

"Pravda," Gregor said.

"You want to wait here, call in the cavalry if I need it, cool with me."

"What fun would that be?"

We had been watching the house for the past hour. It was a two story faux Tudor mansion, the rolling lawn guarded by a tall iron fence. We had circled around the back alley and discovered that that too was covered by an equally formidable fence.

"Bolt cutter?" Gregor said, looking at the locked front gate.

"Not yet."

"What's the plan, boss?"

"We wait." Which we did. Around midnight, there still hadn't been any movement from the house other than a few upstairs windows going dark as the occupants went to sleep. I sent Gregor out for coffee while I slunk down behind an overgrown hedge across the street.

He hadn't been gone five minutes when the black

Mercedes appeared. The giant and Victor were in the front. On the dark street, I couldn't see who was in the back, but I'd bet the ranch whoever it was was lovely, young and partied for a price. They stopped in front of the gate while it slowly rolled open. As they drove in, I ran across the road, slipping through the gate as it slammed closed. Ducking to the right, I pushed in behind a thick line of cypress. I could hear several car doors open from the back of the property, then all went silent. From an inner courtyard, a fountain splashed and the crickets rejoined their song.

"Hey gulla boi, you ready to die?" Victor slipped out from behind a tree, pointed a large automatic at my head.

"Only if you're ready to kill me," I said.

"I think I am... Da, why not." His thumb snapped off the pistol's safety. There was a whistle of wind and a heavy object connected with the back of his bald head. His eyes shot up and his body went limp. As he fell to the ground, I saw Gregor standing behind him with bolt cutters in his hand.

"Can't I leave you alone for one minute, boss?"

"Apparently not." We pulled Victor to his feet. He was groggy and didn't seem to be able to focus his eyes. Slipping his piece into my belt, we dragged him towards the back of the house.

A large shale turnaround separated the house from a free-standing six-car garage.

"Where is Anya?" I asked Victor, slapping his face hard to make sure he was paying attention. His head lolled, indicating a short stone stairwell leading down under the house.

At the bottom landing we found a short hall lit by a

single bulb. A sturdy padlock secured a door at the end of the corridor. Gregor tried the bolt cutters, but the lock must have been made of hardened steel. With a shrug, he applied his boot to the door. The wood splintered in, snapping off a ragged panel that remained attached to the lock. As the door fell open, I tossed Victor through the opening. Guns in hand, we rolled in after him, Gregor went left and I right. On one knee, I swept the room. Cots were lined in three rows, it was a cramped dormitory. The walls were unpainted concrete, beams and floorboards made up the low ceiling. It was the sort of basement you'd expect to find tools and spiders in, instead we found eight beautiful young women. They were sitting or laying on the cots. Our kicking the door in got their attention, but none screamed or showed any real panic at having two armed men burst in on them. On a paint-worn dresser, a black and white TV showed a dubbed version of *Pretty Woman*. Out of Julia Roberts' mouth came the voice of a bored Russian actor.

"Moses?" I hardly recognized Marina, she looked like a child in her flannel pajamas, her makeup scrubbed off. "Why have you come here?"

"What the hell are you doing here?" I asked her.

"You have to leave, now."

Looking past her, I scanned for Anya. Tatyana, the tiny redhead, sat close, burning into me with her cold eyes. "They will kill you for this," she was a broken record.

"Anya?" I called out. Victor started to try and stand up. Gregor knocked him down and whipped a lock tie around his wrists.

Moving down the rows of girls, I found Anya at the back of the basement. Crumpled up into a ball, she seemed to be hiding from me.

"Anya?" I touched her leg and she looked up at me, her eyes full of fear.

"You shouldn't be here," she said, her eyes darting to the other girls.

"You want me to leave?" I said.

"Yes." Her face wasn't as sure as her voice.

"I thought you were in trouble."

"Why? Did I say I was in trouble? No, I did not. Now go." She had gotten up and was pushing me towards the door.

"I guess I'm an idiot."

"Yes. Now go."

"Foolish old man, I thought you were a prisoner. No?"

"No. We are free to come and go as we wish."

"Right, only the lock on the door says different."

"For our protection. The lock keeps us safe."

"From guys like me. Ok, my mistake." I looked from her to the other girls; their fearful sullen faces told me they weren't intending to give us a parade, or jump into our arms with gratitude.

"Alright. Gregor, let's go," I said and walked between the bunks to the doorway.

"How about him?" Gregor stood over Victor.

"Leave him." We were out in the hall when Anya caught

up. Grabbing my arm, she looked into my eyes. A single tear rolled down her cheek.

"You don't understand, I can't go with you." She spoke in a whisper.

"Yeah, you made that clear."

"They have my little sister. If I don't do what they say, they will kill her."

"Get your sister and I'll take you both out of here."

"No, she's..." She let out a sad string of Russian words.

"She says," Gregor translated, "her sister left Russia, but they will not tell her where she is now. The sister's thirteen. She must do whatever they want."

"You think she's being straight?" I whispered to Gregor.

"Yeah, boss, I do. Not the first time I heard shit like this. They took my cousin to Israel, told her she'd be a hotel maid, then threatened to kill her father if she didn't work in their brothel."

"What happened to her?"

"She killed herself," he said.

"Get your things," I told Anya, "We're leaving."

"I can't." Anya's eyes darted back to the dormitory where all the girls were watching us.

"We'll get your sister back, I promise."

"Oh, you promise, that makes all ok? They will kill you and me, and then who will look after Nika?"

"How are you going to take care of her? Call it what you want, but you're a slave."

"Everyone is owned, at least I know who owns me." She wasn't budging. I looked to Gregor for help.

He spoke to her in soft Russian. After a moment, she slowly nodded her head.

"Let's go," Gregor said.

"She coming with us?"

"Of course."

"What'd you say?" I asked him.

"Told her the truth."

"What truth?"

"Told her she was screwed with the men here, they wouldn't believe she didn't bring us. And that we were bad motherfuckers, no Russian pussies are going to take us down."

While she went to collect her things, Gregor and I climbed the steep stairs.

Stepping onto the shale turnaround I saw movement behind us. Spinning around, guns up and ready, we found ourselves facing three AK47s. The giant and two other Russian thugs stood against the house on either side of the stairwell. Gregor flicked his eyes to me, asking if we should go for it, let rip and see how many we could take down before they shredded us. Three full auto assault rifles vs. our pea shooters, odds were a little too lopsided even for a degenerate gambler like me. Dropping the hammer on my .38, I tossed it toward the giant. Gregor let out a grunt of displeasure, then gave up his piece.

The giant told us in Russian to put our hands on our heads. I may not have understood his words, but I knew the drill. After a rough pat search, they moved us through the back door of the mansion, through a kitchen that would make Emeril Lagasse drool, through a dining room with a long oak table and into the whitest room I've ever been in. I guess it was a den or some such. Thick white shag ran up to glossy white baseboards. A horseshoe of white leather couches faced a huge flat panel TV monitor. The screen was showing ten smaller pictures, images from security cameras. In the lower left picture I could see the girls in the basement dormitory. Anya was freeing Victor.

In a large white club chair, facing the screen, sat a man who looked well into his seventies. A fringe of white hair circled his wrinkled bald head. He looked from the monitor to me, his eyes dull and empty. A small smile crept into his lips, but died before it could make it to his eyes.

"What?" I asked.

"You Americans, your stupidity is only matched by your arrogance," the old man said. "Somehow in your tiny reptilian brain, you thought you could stroll onto my land and pilfer my possessions. Can you truly be that dense?"

The question seemed rhetorical, a strike to the back of my head with a rifle barrel told me I was wrong. I stumbled forward, struggling to keep my face neutral.

"Too dull to answer a simple question?" the old man asked. "Let us try one that is a bit more specific: who sent you?"

My lack of an answer was met by another rifle hit. It must have been the giant behind me, because the blow drove me to my knees. Gregor tried to get to me, but two men threw him against the wall, and pinned him there.

"A slow learner, I see," the old man said. "Victor told me you worked for Don Gallico, but I cannot see that as being truthful. If he wanted to send me a message, he would simply pick up the phone, not send a simpleton and his Armenian serving boy. With the tip and a tap, I can turn Gallico's power off and he knows it. So the question remains, who sent you?"

"Fuck off." The rifle butt knocked me flat onto the floor. The middle of my spine burned like it had a hot poker on it.

"Yes, yes, you are quite the deipnosophist. Pasha, kill the Armenian," he said to the giant. When the giant turned to look at Gregor, I rolled onto my back and kicked upward with all I had. The steel toe of my boot connected with his groin. A high pitched shriek burst out of him, along with all the air in his lungs. Rolling to the left, I grabbed the barrel of the rifle that hung loosely in his hand. I swung it like a baseball bat. I could hear the crack of the stock when it struck his head. The giant took two wobbly steps then collapsed onto the floor.

Flipping the AK around, I drew a bead on the old man's forehead. The room went still. The old man's dead eyes opened only slightly. Gregor was still pinned to the wall, one of the goons pressed his rifle into Gregor's eye socket.

"Better tell your punk to release my friend, before I get nervous and this whole deal gets wet," I told the old man.

CHAPTER 6

Slowly, the old man let out a hissing sigh. "We have quite a conundrum here. You appear to have captured the king, checkmate. But what if the king does not mind dying?"

"Then we have one thing in common." I kept the AK trained on his face.

"If you shoot me, they most definitely will shoot him." He tilted his head toward Gregor, who shrugged indifferently. "How delightfully stoic, brave heroes to the end."

"Fuck this noise." Pivoting, I pulled the trigger. Blood exploded from the knee of the man holding a rifle on Gregor. As he fell, Gregor grabbed his second guard by the collar and ran him headfirst into the wall. Before the echo of the shot died, all were down and I again was aimed at the old man. He hadn't moved an inch, he simply watched it go down.

"Nicely played. I seem to have underestimated your brute desire to win," he said.

After Gregor tied the goon squad up, he went down to get Anya. I had a little chat with the old man. If his turn of fortune had shaken him, he sure was hiding it well. "Young man, you have truly stuck your head into the proverbial hornets' nest. The odds of your surviving the next forty-eight hours are less than zero."

"Maybe I should deep six you and walk away."

"That is what I, if in your cheap shoes, would most certainly do. But it would not change your fate. From this moment forth, no hole will be deep enough nor distant enough for you to hide in."

"Where is Anya's sister?"

"Quite honestly, I have no knowledge, nor desire for any, of the girl's whereabouts."

The report of my rifle exploded into the still room. The bullet ripped into the club chair's leather inches from his head, kicking soft tufts of stuffing onto his cheek. He looked from the hole to me without fear.

"Game's over, motherfucker." My ears were ringing from the shot.

"On the contrary, the game is just now beginning. Get your little slut and get off my property, your histrionics are starting to bore me."

I wanted so badly to splatter his smirking face across his lovely chair. But that would be wrong, and more importantly, stupid. Never make a bold play until you know the rules of the game. I had made that mistake by stumbling in here, no need to compound it.

After sweeping the mansion and binding all the occupants, we left through the front door. Anya had emerged from the basement, wearing a deep green velvet dress that made her eyes sparkle. She had matching green heels, expertly applied make-up and her lips shone like fresh washed cherries. Even on the run she wanted to look her best.

At the car, Gregor had me pop the trunk. From under his greatcoat he pulled an AK47.

"A souvenir," he said, and slammed the trunk closed.

"Did they tell you where my sister is?" Anya asked as we drove slowly down the quiet street.

"We'll find her."

"How? What have you done? If she dies, it will be your fault." She was right, of course. Now a thirteen year old girl's life depended on my next move. I needed to buy time, time to think, time to plan. I needed a drink.

Borrowing Gregor's cloned and untraceable cell phone, I called Lowrie at home. He was an LAPD homicide detective, and the only cop I trusted. I roused him from deep slumber, but years on the job trained him to snap to alertness regardless of the hour. After busting my balls for waking him, we got to it. I gave him the mansion's address and told him he would find a basement full of trafficked Russian girls, illegal weapons and hog tied Russian mobsters.

"And this involves homicide how?" he asked.

"Preventive, you don't do something about it, there will be a murder, I'm sure of it."

"But not by you, right?"

"Never, you know me, John Q Law-Abider."

"I have a friend on the Russian mob task force, any chance you'll talk to them?" He already knew the answer but he had to ask.

"I wasn't even there."

"And if the Russians say different?"

"Then they're liars." If they could ID me, I wouldn't have dropped the dime. I told Lowrie I'd call him the next day and clicked off.

We traversed Los Angeles without seeing any black Mercedes, no gun toting mobsters, not even any patrol cars. To be safe, we decided Gregor would camp out at my place. Angel bounced up for a pet from me and then Gregor, who knelt down so she could slime his face. Anya looked anxiously at my big dog. With a snap of my finger I pointed to Angel's dog bed, after fluffing her pillows with her paws, she lay down.

While Gregor made coffee, I poured Anya a tall scotch. The scent made me more than want to pour myself a tall one. She took a long gulp of whisky, then closed her eyes tight. Maybe she was hoping this was a bad dream. If it was, it started long before she met me.

At her feet, a single suitcase held all she owned. Whatever she made dancing hadn't gone in her pocket, she had forty two dollars folding cash and some coins rattling around in her purse. No passport, no driver's license, not a piece of paper to prove she existed. She was off the grid in a foreign land, and now her only hope rested in the hands of a suicidal titty bar bouncer and an Armenian street thug.

"The cops will buy us a couple of days before we show

back up on the Russians' radar, we need to find your sister before they lawyer up and spread the word."

"Nika, that is her name, Nika..." Her eyes were still shut. Her voice came from far off. "Will they kill her?"

"No." That's what I told her, as if I had one fucking clue what was coming next.

While Gregor and I drank coffee and she drank more scotch, I had her tell us how she came to the States. If I could trace her course, I might be able to find her sister. Anya had flown from Moscow to Israel and then Mexico. They had customs officers on the mob's paysheet.

"I was not foolish enough to believe I was coming here to be a maid. My eyes were, as you say, wide open. But back home, there was no hope. Here, I could make real money, buy a better life. Such a mistake." Her eyes clenched tight to keep the tears from falling.

"After the airport, where did you go?"

"They took me to a house, away from the city. Other girls were with me, we hadn't eaten in days..." Tears rolled and she went silent.

"It's alright, you can tell me," I said.

She looked to Gregor, imploring him in Russian.

"She's afraid you won't want her if you know what they did to her. You'll think she is damaged goods. Her words, not mine, boss. I told her we were all damaged goods in this room."

"He's right," I told her. "How long did they keep you in the house?"

"A long time, weeks, I don't know." She was crying now with abandon, snot ran down her lip. Black lines of mascara streaked down from her eyes. The humanness of it made me want to protect her from this screwed up world. Gregor handed her a linen handkerchief. In the face of pain, he neither shied away nor reveled in it. He'd simply respond.

Anya wiped her face, blew her nose and smiled at Gregor. "I stained it, I'm sorry."

"It's not important," he said, followed by Russian. She answered him, but I was clueless to what they were saying. He continued to soothe her, her tears slowed, she even smiled at something he said.

I dropped an army surplus sleeping bag, a comforter and a couple of pillows onto the sofa. "Shall I sleep with you?" Anya asked, looking nervously from Gregor to me.

"You don't owe me anything."

"But if I choose to?"

"Sweet, but no." I snapped my finger and Angel followed me to bed. Laying there, I felt like a fucking idiot. Ten feet away was a woman offering to give herself to me. A woman I could love. Not like this. I wanted to prove myself to her, prove I was worthy to be her man. She would come to me when she was strong and unafraid, and I would be more than just a thug she needed for protection. I fell asleep to the foreign murmur coming from the living room.

It was just past seven the next morning when I slipped out of the house with Angel at my side. Anya was sleeping on the sofa, snoring softly, in a sweet girlish way. Gregor looked up at me from the chair by the door where he had spent the night, he didn't ask where I was going. He scratched Angel between the ears and watched us leave.

Picking up some pan dulce from the Mexican bakery down the street we hit the dog park. Angel's best friend was Bruiser, a Rottweiler that had thoroughly kicked her ass as a puppy. Now at a little over a year old, they were evenly matched as they did their impression of WWF.

"When she fills out, he's going to be sorry he wasn't nicer when she was young." Helen laughed, wiping away the crumbs of sugary Mexican pastry from her mouth.

"Fills out? Why didn't you tell me I was taking in a damn horse?" Angel tackled Bruiser, flipping him onto his back. She was more into pinning and wrestling than biting.

Helen was forty-five, sloppy and overweight. If she wasn't a friend, I'd have said she was built like a mushroom, as it was, I'd kick anyone's ass who put her down. She spent too many hours at her computer writing T.V. scripts and too few in the real world. She was smart and witty and the first citizen to treat me like a human. We were brought together by the death of a girl we had both loved in our own ways. After it was done and I'd made the killers pay their freight, Helen and I stayed friends. I guess because we liked each other. Strange, a friendship where nothing was exchanged or bartered.

"You are so not a dog guy. Angel won't hit her full size until she's two years old. Did you read the book I gave you on Mastiffs or is it keeping your kitchen table from wobbling?"

"It was pretty wobbly." I grinned at her.

"You suck, you know that Moses? You totally and fully suck."

"But I bring you pan dulce and my silly bitch keeps Bruiser young."

"Both good points." She watched our dogs suddenly break from a huddle and burst across the park like two fur bullet trains. "And we have shared history, and that is worth more and more as the clock ticks by."

"Sadie?" I asked.

"Left last night. And don't insult me with sham surprise. I know she was too young for me, but damn she was..."

"Yes she was, Helen, yes she was." Sadie had been her latest girlfriend. She was fine, twenty-five with a runner's body. Not the kind that was too skinny and dehydrated looking. Muscular down deep, with just enough flesh covering it to make you think she would be soft to curl into.

"You think some people are meant to be alone?" Helen asked.

"I don't know if I'm the guy to ask. My longest relationship is with that dog over there. But no, babe, I don't think you're meant to be alone. Don't think anything is meant to be. It just is what it is."

"Not into predestination?"

"Whatever the fuck that is," I said a bit harder than I should have.

"Fate, destiny, the belief that our lives are planned by some higher force and we mere mortals live them out the best we can with the limited knowledge we have."

"Oh, that predestination. No, I don't believe some higher force is planning this life for me. If I did, I'd give up, lay down and die right now. Because it would be clear, that fuck in the sky hates my ass."

"You are in a darker mood than usual, Moses. And what is up with the bags under your eyes?" She looked at me with true concern.

"You know me, if there's any shit in a ten mile radius, I will step in it."

"And what shit is it this time?"

"Do you know anything about the Russian mob trafficking women?" I knew she would, or would know where to find it. Most of her writing was on crime shows, and she was one hell of a researcher.

"This is why you came to me, right? Bribe me with some pan dulce to do your leg work?"

"There's a girl, thirteen, I think she's somewhere in Mexico. I have to find her."

"No, you have to go to the feds. These Russians, they kill cops, judges, they make you look like a pansy," she said.

"Clock is ticking on this little girl. I don't have time for the feds. The war on terror is still the only thing they have on the brain, one Russian girl won't even be a shadow of a blip on their screen." I looked at her solemnly. "Can you help?"

"Damn it, Moses, these people don't play around."

"Neither do I."

"Ok, alright, give me a day. I'll see what's on the web, call a few contacts."

"Thank you." Pulling Angel off Bruiser, I headed back to Highland Park.

CHAPTER 7

Nika let the rumble of the tires on the road lull her, she lay back using her bag as a lumpy pillow. Her first day in this new world was spent locked in back of a sweltering, windowless van. Three other girls traveled with her. Two were from Ukraine, the third came all the way from Norilsk, up in the permanently frozen north. They had spoken in the dark - trying to keep their courage up - all agreed this wasn't as bad as it could be. Soon they would walk onto the wonderful streets of America. They passed a jug of water, but there was no food. Their sweat and cheap perfume mixed in the stale air.

"Hey Moscow, what the fuck are you doing?" Yumma asked. At nineteen, she was the oldest of the girls, she had the thick gravel in her voice that only years of tobacco can give.

"It's Yaroslavl." Nika twisted, unzipping her dress.

"I don't care fuck where you're from, keep your dress on. You want them to think we're whores?"

"I'm hot, and you're not my mother."

"Thank god for that. Do any of you useless cows have a

cigarette?"

Nika pulled the dress over her head. In her slip, she felt much better. After a long, hot moment, she heard the zippers of other girls following her lead.

"Oh, that's real classy. What will they think when they open the door and find you idiots naked?"

Twenty minutes later, Nika smiled when she heard Yumma's zipper slowly go down.

Lunch hour came and went without a break. In the afternoon the van stopped and they could hear a loud tinny radio playing brassy music. None of the girls spoke Spanish, the rapid speech of the DJ was a blur of noise to them. They heard the gas tank filling. Nika knocked on the door, pleading that she needed to pee.

Blinding light filled their compartment. Glowing in the sun, the man with the acne-ruined face tossed a plastic bucket in to them. Before Nika's eyes could adjust enough to make out the surroundings, the door banged closed again. It embarrassed her to squat over the bucket, but it was either that or have her bladder burst. The sound of her urine splashing down caused one of the girls to giggle.

"What?" Nika snapped. She had no idea which girl it was, but she would be damned if they would laugh at her.

"Sorry." It was Guzel Saifutdinova, the girl from Norilsk. Nika could tell by her small mouse like voice. It was as if she thought even in their dark cage, someone would overhear her.

Nika felt a little better having lost the pain of a swollen bladder. It was the most satisfying piss she had ever had. Strange, she thought, how denying a thing can make it so much better once you got it.

"I'm hungry." This came from the deep voiced Zhanna. She had told them she was seventeen and came from Odessa. She had been studying for her college entrance exams when her mother lost her job at the Volga automobile factory. With no money or hope, she decided to leave for America.

"Here," Nika said. On the plane, she had slipped saltines and peanuts into her bag. "No cigs, huh?" Yumma said.

"No. Have a cracker, pretend it's a smoke." Nika shared her snacks with the others. Why not, soon they would have to stop for dinner. The man driving the van wouldn't starve them.

They didn't stop for dinner. Nika's stomach was growling when she finally let sleep take her away. How long she slept was impossible to tell. The combination of jet lag and the monotony of the dark van left her disoriented. A knot had tightened in her belly, from both fear and hunger. The van had turned from oppressive heat to bone chilling cold. The girls huddled together, wrapping the rough Mexican blankets around themselves.

"We never should've come here," Guzel whined, near tears. "If I wanted to freeze to death, I could have stayed home. Where are they taking us? We don't even know who they are. This was a terrible mistake."

"Shhh, we'll be alright," Nika said.

"How do you know? They can do what they want with us, who will protect us?"

"Why would they fly us across the world to hurt us?" Nika was sounding much braver than she felt. "I don't know how it was in Norilsk, but in Yaroslavl it sucked."

Guzel sobbed quietly.

"Stop crying." Nika grabbed the girl's shoulder and shook her roughly. Guzel fell silent. Nika lay back down, pulling up her blanket. Since her big sister left home, she had been forced to grow up. She took over the household. It was her job to keep her father in line, or he would spend what little money they had on wine.

At thirteen, Nika was the youngest in the van, but now she was the one they turned to for leadership. If she had to be harsh to keep them from falling apart, she would. With every step, from Yaroslavl to Moscow to Mexico, she had faced new fears, and with each conquered she felt braver. Whatever came next, she would deal with it. And in the end, she was sure the prize in America would prove to be worth it.

"The phone's been ringing off the hook," Gregor said when I returned.

"Who called?"

"Who knows? Boss, everyone has an answering machine. I could hook you up."

I should have guessed he wouldn't answer it. I hadn't asked him to, and why would I, the damn thing never rang. Before I could ask him where Anya was, the phone started ringing.

"Where the hell have you been?" It was a seriously not happy Detective Lowrie.

"Out. What bug crawled up your ass?"

"I'm running on two hours of sleep and paranoia, so don't screw with me."

"Ok, but I can't answer questions you're not asking."

"Who the fuck did you piss off?"

"Excuse me?" I felt like I was caught in some bizarre hidden camera show.

"I call my man in the Russian mob squad, twenty minutes later I have some cowboy with a Homeland Security badge at my door."

"A fed?"

"Yeah, a big fat G-man. He wanted your name and kept throwing terms like 'enemy combatant' like it was confetti and the Lakers had won the title."

"You give me up?"

"Screw him."

"Thanks."

"Didn't do it for you, I can't stand anyone coming into my playground and telling me the bat and ball are theirs."

"What's their interest here?"

"Hell if I know, I was kind of hoping you might shed some light on this bullshit."

"No idea. Did the Russians say anything to the Mob Squad?" I asked.

"Hell, they never even rolled on it. My guy said the house was on a federal 'don't touch' list. Is that pure crap or what?"

My mind spun. If the Russian mobsters weren't in lockdown, then they would be out hunting us. They didn't know my name, and even if they did, I paid cash for my rent and the utilities were in the owner's name. If you didn't know me, finding me was next to impossible.

"Odds are real good the captain's going to be on my ass to give up my snitch, and that's you," Lowrie said.

"Give me twenty-four hours and I'll be smoke."

"Tell me it's for a good cause."

"A thirteen year old girl has been trafficked. I have to find her before the Russians do."

I could hear his breath as he exhaled into the phone. After a thought-filled moment he finally said in a flat measured tone, "I'll give you what I can."

"Thank you." I knew he would do what he could, and that was the most I could expect of any man.

I was about to fill Gregor in when Anya stepped out of the bathroom. Wet from a shower, she was dressed only in a towel. I had to control my jaw from dropping. Fresh, clean, without makeup, she looked years younger and made me feel years older for lusting after her.

Gregor looked from her to me, then got up and went into the kitchen.

"Where did you go?" Anya asked, moving up to me as if she were unaware of the affect she was having on me. I watched a bead of water roll over her collar bone and down her chest. She watched my eyes, and smiled softly.

"You are going to find my sister, yes?"

"Yes." The phone rang, saving me from falling into Anya's

eyes.

"Moses, things have gone crazy down here." It was Piper and she sounded uncharacteristically rattled. "They tore this place up, broken bottles, booze all over the floor. Put Turaj in the hospital."

"Slow down, darlin', who tore it up?" I asked

"I got here early, Turaj was setting up, I was in the dressing room. I heard shouting and stayed hid. What kind of mental midget robs a strip club before it opens?"

"They robbed the club?" Even stone cold idiots knew we took the cash to the bank every night, all we ever had at the beginning of a shift was a couple hundred for change.

"You know, I forgot to ask them what they were doing there, I was a little busy crawling into the back of a closet."

"You didn't see anything?"

"Got a good look at the back of the closet. Did you know one of the girls keeps a box of dope and a pipe back there?"

"Real interesting. Where's Uncle Manny?"

"Glendale Adventist, that's where the paramedics took Turaj."

"Paramedics?" Turaj was the club owner's nephew and a worthless womanizer, but if anyone was going to fuck him up I wanted it to be me.

"They hurt him bad. What the hell is going on, Mo?"

"I don't know. Call Doc, tell him to get his black ass in there, then call Jesus and see if he can put together a cleaning crew.

Have them restock the bar. I'll find Uncle Manny and see if he wants us to open." Piper was much calmer when she hung up. The girls might mock me, think I was a jerk and a joke, but when the shit hit, I was always the first they'd call.

"Gregor," I called out, "stay put, and watch the door."

"What's up, boss?" He came out of the kitchen carrying a fry pan he was drying.

"When I know, I'll call, so pick up." I was out the door at a run.

Uncle Manny was pacing in the surgical waiting room. Fereshteh, Manny's wife, sat quietly with her head bowed. I had never met her, but recognized her immediately from the family photo Manny kept on his desk.

"Moses?" Uncle Manny looked surprised to see me.

"Where's Turaj?"

"Come." Uncle Manny nodded his head out of the room. He led me through the hospital and out onto a small smoking balcony.

"Do you have a cigarette?" It was the first he had spoken since leaving his wife.

"Quit years ago," I told him.

"Me too." His eyes were rimmed with red, and he looked old.

"Who did it, Manny?"

"This is none of your concern."

"Bullshit. Someone comes in my club, fucks with my people, it's my business."

"It is not your club. It is my club, and I'm telling you to stay out of it." His voice was flat and devoid of emotion.

"Was it the Russians?"

"Go home, Moses. This is family trouble, I will handle it." Without meeting my eyes he turned and walked back into the hospital.

Walking to my car, it hit me. How fucking stupid could one man be? In the mansion, we trussed up the old man and his thugs, but we left the girls free. They may have hated the mutants who held them captive, but without passports, or any cash, the girls didn't have a lot of options. I made sure the Russians didn't know my name, but Marina sure as hell knew my name and where I worked. If she sold me out to save her own skin, I didn't blame her, I blamed myself for not thinking of it. Now Turaj was in surgery, he had taken the weight meant for me. Whether he gave me up straight away or they beat it out of him, fact was, I was sure they had my address.

Running to a pay phone, I fumbled two quarters in and dialed home. The phone rang fifteen times before I clicked off.

I parked around the corner from my house, I took my 1911 .45 from the tire well, slipped it in my belt and moved quickly along the sidewalk. An empty black Mercedes was at the curb. Keeping their car between me and the house, I crouched down by the fender. It takes more force than most think to slit a tire, even with a razor honed buck knife. The air escaped with a crisp hiss. I peeked over the hood, but nothing moved in the house.

Slipping along the side yard, I stole a glance into the bedroom. It was free of Russian dick heads. With a Bullmastiff as an alarm, I had taken to leaving my windows open. Pulling up onto the sill, I dropped silently to the floor. From the living room or kitchen, I heard several men speaking in Russian. I needed to cross the open doorway to get to the closet, and the hidden cabinet where I kept the big guns. Holding my breath, I took one long step across the opening. Pinned against the wall, I waited for them to come running. But they kept talking in the same casual tone.

Sliding my hanging clothes aside, I pushed the spring lock on the cabinet set into the back wall. The lock popped much louder than I had hoped. The conversation in the living room stopped abruptly. Footsteps moved quickly toward the bedroom. I grabbed the first gun my hand hit, my Mossberg 12-gauge street sweeper.

The first man through the door was a tanned muscle boy, he was sweeping the room with a small automatic when I rolled out of the closet. From the floor I fired up, the blast of buckshot took him in the chest and sent him doing the rag doll tumble into the living room.

Racking a fresh shell in, I fired through the open door. Noise and gun smoke filled the small room. Crawling back into the closet, I grabbed my battle bag. It was a duffle I always kept packed and ready with cash, false and real ID, a change of clothes, my handguns and enough ammunition to end a small war.

My bedroom exploded in a hail of bullets. Several Russians swung into the doorway and emptied their pistols, bullets pocked the walls and ripped my mattress to shreds. Shards from a mirror mixed with the spent shells hitting the floor. If I hadn't been in the closet, I surely would have died in the blitz.

The noise stopped as quickly as it started. When they ducked out to reload, I leapt up. Firing one aimless shot at the living room, I dropped the Mossberg and dove out the ruined window. Rolling when I hit the soft earth, I jumped to my feet and started running. Hitting the Crown Vic, I stomped on the gas and burned two black lines in the asphalt halfway up the block. It wasn't until I hit Eagle Rock Boulevard that I let off on the pace.

Parking in Foster Freeze's lot, I listened for sirens. Thankfully, my home was in Highland Park, it would take the cops at least twenty minutes to respond if the neighbors even bothered to call it in. Down here, we take care of our own, and keep our mouths and eyes shut when it comes to the cops.

The adrenaline eased off enough to lower the thump in my ears to a dull roar. What had happened to Gregor and Anya? If they were in the house and still alive, I doubted the Russians would have been talking so calmly. Fuck! If Angel was there, she would have run to me when I crept in. If those freaks killed my dog, I would paint the walls with their blood.

Jamming into reverse, I squealed out onto the street. I was flying, rage driven, when I rounded the hill that separated Eagle Rock from Highland Park. The Vic slid around the sweeping corners in a four wheel drift.

Victor was kneeling by the Mercedes' front passenger tire. He was finishing tightening the lug nuts on the spare. His head jerked up when he heard me roaring down on him. He leapt up just in time to meet my grille. His legs flipped forward and his chest slammed down onto my hood. He left a face sized dent where his head smashed down. I stamped my foot down, locking up the massive brakes, and Victor rolled, tumbling off the hood and onto the pavement.

Pulling my .45 I jumped out. I didn't bother checking Victor, his threat factor had surely hit zero. The rest of the Russian crew were piled into the Mercedes. Spinning backwards, they bumped over the jack. Standing in the middle of the street, I popped off all seven shots in the clip as they sped away. Their windshield spider-webbed as the bullets struck it. They were gone too soon for me to know if I hit any of the occupants, but I didn't have any time to worry about them. The cops would be rolling. Even Highland Park has its limits, and emptying a clip in the street, I was sure I had crossed them.

I took the four steps up to my door in one big leap. Running from room to room, I searched for signs of death. If they had killed Gregor, Anya or my dog, they had done a damn clean job of it. Picking up the Mossberg, I heard the soft wail of sirens coming on fast. It was time to jet. Pulling down the blinds, I deadbolted the front door behind me.

After policing up the .45 shells off the road, I grabbed the twisted and broken Victor and tossed him into the back seat. I drove quickly away from the oncoming cop cars. He was bitching and moaning in Russian as I took a series of sharp turns, losing myself in the hills of Mount Washington.

Pulling behind a tall wild bramble on an empty hillside lot, I killed the engine. Slapping in a fresh clip, I racked a shell into the .45 and pointed it over the seat at Victor. "Where the fuck are they?" I said, fighting the urge to splatter him.

"Who... I don't know..." He was mumbling through clenched teeth.

I struck his broken arm with the barrel of my .45. His scream sounded more animal than human. "Motherfucker. Talk or die, I don't give a fuck which." I shoved his head down with the pistol.

"No!" His eyes were wild with pain and fear.

"What did you do with my people?" I tapped his head hard with the pistol, to be sure I had his full attention.

"No one... we found no one," he said between moans.

"Wrong answer." I covered my face with my free hand to avoid getting blow-back gore in my eyes.

"Pravda! No one!" His panicked fear was overriding his pain. I dropped the .45 into my lap. Down in the valley, the sounds of sirens had died out. There would be no going home now that it was a crime scene. I could only hope they wouldn't link me to the house and put out an APB.

It was time to go off the map, slip into the unregistered world where cash was king and all names were false. The Russian mobsters would be hunting me with deep vengeance in their hard little hearts, the cops might be looking for me, the feds were in the wings someplace and I was no closer to finding Anya's sister.

I pulled Victor out of the car on a side street near Glendale Adventist, it wouldn't take long for a doctor or ambulance to find him crumpled in the middle of the street. I didn't give a rat's ass if he died, he had brought this crap to my home and he paid the price. Maybe I should have put one in his brain pan and left him in the hills, but I knew the truth of violence. The first life I took was in Beirut. I killed a woman in a fire fight. It was a mistake, doesn't change the fact she was dead at my hand. I learned that moment that every life you take pulls a piece of you with them into the grave.

CHAPTER 8

I stay in the shadows. Work my way along the dock. There is the stink of diesel. Rotting fish. Salt brine coming off the Sea of Cortez. Bass thumps through the walls of the wharf dives. Above a strip club, a ruby neon woman bends and drops her top, over and over and over.

"You looking for to get laid, mister?" He is slick. Shiny long hair pulled back into a ponytail. Several silver and gold crosses hang from his neck. They will not protect him.

"I'm looking for a girl." All trace of the Ukraine are gone. I speak Spanish, but to him, I speak English. My North American accent passes.

"Sure, I get you cherry pussy. What chu like, big, little, skinny schoolgirl, fat mamacita, I got 'em all."

"Russian, I want a Russian girl. You have any?"

The pimp stares at my face. I feel his eyes trace the scar, the jagged line from my left eye down across my cheek all the way to my chin. "Does it frighten you?"

"What, I'm no afraid, is bueno."

"You look afraid." His eyes dart around, looking for help that will be too late. "Do you know who I am?" Stories are told of me across Mexico and Israel. Many think they are myths made up by the Mafia to scare independent operators out of the flesh trade. He has just figured out they are true.

"It's you."

"Yes, it is." I back him deeper into the alley. This pimp tries to get to the blade in his pocket only to find his arm going limp. He didn't feel the straight razor slice through his biceps. Blood flows down, quickly soaking the sleeve of his white coat. He holds the wound. He tries to staunch the flow. There is too much blood to be stopped.

"Tell me about Russian girls."

"Chinga tu..." He steps forward. I drop low, sweep in a circle on my heels. My arm strikes out. The blade slices cleanly through the tendons behind his right knee. Like a puppet gone slack, the pimp crumples onto cobblestone.

"If you know who I am, then you know you are going to die. Who has Russian girls in La Paz?"

"No one, nada, Gordo G had, but no more. They take them to Ensenada. Swear." His skin grows pale. A red lake forms under him.

"Say your prayers." Turning away, I gave him a moment to mumble his last words.

I slash his throat. Clean. I find a small roll of pesos in his blood soaked pockets. I take rings and watch off his limp hands. I leave the crucifixes on his neck. I am careful not to slip on the gore. I drop the tarot card onto his body. I wipe my hands on my jeans. I pull the collar of my jacket up, its dark fabric hides the blood splatter.

And across the Sea of Cortez, a van entered Ensenada. It was early evening, Nika knew, because the stale air around her was starting to cool off. Two days without food had left her weak and dizzy. Dreams and reality washed against each other. She lay with Anya on the bank of the Volga, sipping fruit juice and laughing at the boys showing off for the girls. A string bean with a shock of white blonde hair cannonballed into the icy water. Anya started to speak to her in Spanish. Nika tried to tell her she didn't understand, but her sister kept rambling with ever increasing speed. The van hit a bump, and the Volga dissolved into a rolling cave. In the shadows, Nika could hear the rumbling growls and gnashing teeth of unseen beasts as they circled her.

Passing a plaza, mariachi music dulled by the van's walls mixed with children's laughter and male whoops. The crackle of fireworks pulled Nika back into her body. She gathered her dress against the coming chill. The sounds of the plaza faded as they drove to the outskirts of town. After another twenty minutes of rutted twisting road, they came to a stop. The driver got out, rocking the van slightly on its shocks. A chain rattled and then large pieces of metal could be heard scraping against earth. The cab's door slammed shut and they drove up a steep incline. The girls had to hold on to the side panels to keep from sliding into the back door.

The van skidded to a stop on gravel. Iron hinges creaked, a heavy wooden gate closed behind them. The van's back door opened, cool blue moonlight spilled in on the girls. They were tattered and worn out, like flowers the week after Valentine's Day. Nika stumbled forward, almost falling when she stepped from the van. Without warning, a blurred beast charged Nika.

"Wolf!" a deep voice yelled. Inches before the dog's razor teeth connected with the girl, it stopped. "Down!" the master called, and the beast dropped onto its belly. Its yellow eyes watched the girl by the van, but it dared not move.

Nika swayed on her feet, but didn't scream or fall. They were in a large courtyard surrounded on three sides by an adobe hacienda, the final side blocked by an eight foot wooden gate. Sure that the canine threat had passed, Yumma and Zhanna crawled out behind Nika. Guzel, the mouse, stayed curled with her back pressed against the cab. Nika called for her to come out, but she didn't look up.

The pockmarked man came around the van, looking the three girls over with unhidden disgust. "Where's the little one?" he demanded in Russian.

Nika was the only one to meet his eyes. Her stare was met with a cuff that sent her sprawling onto the gravel. The beast lifted its snout, sniffing at her hungrily.

"You have to learn to answer when asked a question."

"You didn't give me time." This time, he hit the back of her head. Instinctively, Nika reared up, ready to fight. Smashing his fist into her face, she tumbled backward. Tears ran down her face. When he stood over her, she looked up with undisguised hatred.

He pulled back his foot, readying to kick the shit out of this insolent girl.

"Zhenya!" A woman's voice froze his foot mid-swing. A large woman in her mid-fifties, waddled across the courtyard. Shooing the man away from Nika, she leaned down. "Oh, my little flower, what has that brute done to you?" Softly, the woman brushed the hair out of Nika's eyes. "Men can be so cruel, did he scare you?"

Nika nodded her head slowly.

"You needn't be afraid, Svetlana is here to take care of you." Helping Nika to her feet, Svetlana moved to inspect the other girls, stroking their hair and lifting their faces up so their eyes met hers. "Oh, what lovely girls you are. And where is your friend?"

"She won't come out, she's afraid," Nika said.

"I see, very well. Who's hungry?" All three girl's faces lit at this. "Don't tell me he didn't feed you. Men! Come follow me." As they passed the pockmarked Zhenya, Svetlana motioned slightly toward the van. The movement was so subtle that Nika thought she had imagined seeing it. As they reached the hacienda's front door, Nika heard a squeal and turned to see Guzel being dragged from the van by her feet. She was clawing at the metal floor, fighting for purchase. With a yank, the man pulled her free. Guzel's head hit the ground, her cry turned to a whimper. Before Nika could see more, the girls were pulled in through the door. The smell of frying meat and warm bread obliterated all feelings except hunger.

To the left of the entryway was a large open dining room, around a long plank table sat twelve heavy wooden chairs. An ornate wrought iron chandelier bathed the room in golden candlelight. Several men sat, eating and talking. Between them, the table was piled with platters of steaming sliced beef, potatoes, squashes of every color, bowls of fresh fruit, bottles of red wine and vodka.

Nika's mouth was watering as she stumbled towards the

dining room. Svetlana caught her elbow and steered her to the right, away from all the wonderful food and through a grand sitting room. With its large leather sofas and ironwork, it looked much like it had when the early Dons built the hacienda. Nika walked with her head turned back, watching the dinner disappear behind her.

"Come, little one," Svetlana said, "I'll find you a nice bed to lay on and then bring you dinner. Relax, dears, your troubles are over."

The bedroom was at the back of the building. Five beds were the only furniture in the bare room. The walls were thick, dingy white adobe. There were no windows, the door was solid and heavy, when it was closed, all sounds of the outer house vanished. When Svetlana left to get dinner, they heard her turn the bolt in the door, locking them in.

"See. I told you it was going to work out," Zhanna said, flopping down on one of the beds.

"You stupid twat," Yumma snapped. Two days without a cigarette had left her nerves jangled and her mood rotten. "You think everything's fine?"

"Svetlana won't let them hurt us. Tell her, Nika."

"Leave me out of it." Nika lay back, closing her eyes.

"We will be fine," Zhanna said.

"Guzel? Will she be fine? She's taking a sauna, they're feeding her grapes?" Yumma flipped her bleached hair back and started a mirthless laugh. "Maybe they took her into town for ice cream and cake."

"Shut up, Yumma," Nika said.

"Make me."

Nika didn't have the focus or energy to take any more shit. Pulling herself off the bed, she looked up at Yumma, who had six inches and at least forty pounds on her. Nika invaded the tall girl's air space, her jaw was firm, her eyes hard.

Yumma broke eye contact first. "Screw you."

Nika relaxed the tension in her face and suddenly started to laugh.

"What?" Zhanna asked, wondering if Nika had cracked.

"My first year at school," Nika said still laughing, "a big girl beat me up. I went to my sister and told her, and she spanked me. Told me she would do it every day until I kicked the girl's ass."

"And that's funny, why?"

Yumma started to chuckle, "Me too, only it was my mother. No dinner until you take that girl down."

"You're both crazy," Zhanna said.

An hour later the lock finally turned and Svetlana came in with a tray filled with food. She hadn't taken two steps in when Kolya stormed past her. He was a stocky older man in a velour jogging suit.

"What the fuck are you doing?" He knocked the tray from Svetlana's hand.

"The girls are hungry."

"Fuck them. They want to eat, they work. They don't want to work, they can starve." He kicked the fallen food into the hallway. After giving Svetlana a chilling glance, he walked out.

"I'm so sorry, men are pigs and Kolya is the worst. But he is the boss. I have to do what he says." The girls looked at her, scared into silence.

"What does he want us to do?" Nika asked in almost a whisper.

"It is nothing, really. Men come here, fellow Russians, nice men, lonely. They pay us to spend time with pretty girls like you." She made it sound innocent, almost a charity.

"And are we supposed to sleep with these men?" Nika asked.

"We are all women here, I can speak frankly. Which one of you hasn't slept with a man because he was cute, or had a car, or could afford to buy you dinner and a night on the town? This is the same, you'll see. Men are pigs and they want what we have, so why not charge them." She left for a moment and returned with a washbasin, a water jug and fresh towels. "Clean yourselves and I will return for you in ten minutes."

After the door locked, Zhanna burst into tears.

"She's right," Yumma said. "When I fucked Vadic, all he bought me was dinner. If I don't like the man, I'll tell him to fuck off. Svetlana wouldn't make us screw a guy we didn't want to."

"You think?" Zhanna said, wiping her eyes.

"Sure." Yumma splashed water on her face, dropped her dress off her shoulders and cleaned her pits. Slowly Zhanna joined her. Nika sat on her bed, not moving, watching them.

"Come on, Nika, you don't want to stink up the place," Yumma said.

"I'm not going," Nika said.

"You have to eat."

"No."

"What if they are cute, and sweet?" Yumma asked.

"I don't care."

"What, you're a virgin?"

"Yes."

"Oh," Yumma said, "it's no big deal, really. All you have to do is lay there. The man does all the work."

"I'm not going," Nika said.

When Svetlana returned, she took notice of Nika but said nothing, as if she had been expecting her to refuse. She led the other two out and locked Nika in. The lights went out and Nika was left in the dark with her hunger and fear.

CHAPTER 9

"Relax, your fucking dog is fine," Piper said. We were sitting in the beast in the back parking lot of Club Xtasy. After finding Gregor's apartment empty, I had gone to her. "Oh yeah, and Gregor and the Russian skirt are ok, too. By the way, are you fucking her or is Gregor?"

"No one's fucking anyone."

"That's a shame."

"Tell me about it."

"If you're not getting laid, then why are you tangled up in this mess?"

"Where are they?"

"Gregor called me, they're laying low over at his mother's place, he gave me the address. Now are you going to tell me what the hell you've got into?"

"Long story."

"Will it have a happy ending?"

"I doubt it." I filled her in, the short version, meeting Anya, the lap dance, the way she made me feel. I kept it simple.

"She must be good," Piper laughed, "to convince an old cynic like you that she actually had the big O."

"I don't think she faked that."

"Men never do, and you are a man. So you had a couch tumble, fell in love and now mobsters are trying to kill you. No, don't explain it. It makes perfect sense in Moses World. You do know it is possible to fall in love without people ending up dead?"

"Didn't say I was in love with her."

"No, but you're willing to risk life, limb and Gregor to save her and the baby sister. What's that sound like to you?"

"Stupidity."

"Exactly, or in other words, love."

"Her little sister, she's lost. Nobody will give a fuck if she lives, dies or anything in between."

"And if you weren't trying to get with the big sister, you'd still care?"

"Yes."

"We have plenty of kids in trouble right here in LA, if it's sainthood you're aiming at."

"I don't know them, their stories. Hers, I do. If I don't do something about it, I'm no better than the freaks who have her."

Piper understood, even if she didn't admit it. She and I didn't vote, picket, donate to save the children, we just did what we could for those we met and left the big picture to those with grander visions than ours. She gave me Gregor's mother's address and a warm kiss goodbye. For a moment as her lips pressed on mine, I wondered when I was going to come to my senses and fall for her. Then again, even with all her flirting, she knew me too well to ever make the mistake of falling for me.

Gregor's mother lived in a California bungalow court off Broadway in Glendale. The small house smelled of boiled meat, cabbage and fresh baked bread. Gregor pulled me in the door, looking around to be sure we were free of prying eyes. His mother knew nothing of our troubles, he wanted to make sure I kept it that way.

"Those Russian fucks showed up at your place. I should have stayed, taken them out. I was worried about Anya."

"You did right."

"No."

"I'm alive, you're alive, Anya's alive. You did fine. I want you to stay here while I get us a clean car and try and figure out what the hell we've stumbled into."

"We're going to find Nika."

"Yeah, we'll find her."

From the path outside, I looked in through the kitchen window. Angel was curled up on the floor, gnawing on a bone at the feet of a small plump woman. Anya was chopping carrots into a bowl. She was wearing a large denim shirt that came down to her knees, it had never looked that good on me. Maybe it was the domestic setting, or the lack of makeup and spike heels, but all the sense of stripper was gone. She was a beautiful young woman, the kind you took home to mother, if your mother wasn't a gin-swilling Jesus freak. I knew, looking at her, I could wake up every morning, roll over, see her and count myself a lucky man.

Gregor came into the kitchen, snatching a bite out of the salad Anya was making. She slapped his hand playfully and they both started laughing. I walked quickly away before I could convince myself I should stay.

I called Helen, my friend from the dog park. She had someone for me to meet. The pink light of sunset was sparkling off the Silver Lake reservoir as I rolled into the hills.

"Bottom line? You could stumble around Ensenada for months and never find their safe house." Peter Brixon, an LA

Times reporter, was sitting across from me in the breakfast nook in Helen's home.

"And taking you with me will do what?" I asked.

"A, I speak Spanish, helpful when in Mexico. B, I've spent the last year investigating Russian sex trafficking, so we won't be starting from zero." He spoke in a rapid clipped way that reminded me of a meth freak two grams into a bad bender.

"Rolling with a punk civilian, looking for his shot at a Pulitzer, is an easy way to get dead."

"Moses, don't be such a prick," Helen interjected, "Peter came here to help you."

"No, he's right," Peter said. "You want my credentials? Fine. Somalia riots, Haiti coup, in Afghanistan I was embedded with Air Cav. Now do I strip down, compare bullet scars to prove I'm no fucking cherry?"

I looked from him to Helen. "I like him. If he walks like he talks, he may survive."

I had only one stipulation and it was a deal breaker: he could come along, he could write his story, I didn't even care if he turned it into a million dollar movie deal, but he wasn't to use my name. Not in the paper, not with cops if it went wrong, not even to his favorite girl. Never. I didn't need the heat that came flooding in with a little notoriety.

While Peter went to pack, I dropped the Crown Vic with Jason B, he was a part-time actor and full-time gear head. He had started a business buying used cop cars and selling them on eBay. But he discovered the real green was in building sleepers for people who needed to run fast and attract as little attention as possible. I had steered illicit business his way, and had hooked him up with a connection for cheap parts of questionable origin. I figured he owed me a solid.

"This lil' sweetie had a blueprinted 454 that delivers an honest 400 horses to the rear tires. But she ain't cheap." He was showing me a mid-sixties International Harvester Scout, the light blue paint was sun bleached almost to white, where it wasn't gray from bondo and primer. The chrome was pitted and the upholstery was more duct tape than fabric. It was perfect.

"How are the papers?" I asked him.

"They'll survive a Smokey stop and snoop, but if they dig into the VINs, you're fucked." He was handsome in a tan, chiseled leading man way, as well as he could sling bullshit, I wondered why he hadn't made it in Hollywood.

"What'll a week cost me?"

"Does this look like Avis? Do I look like I try harder? This beauty is forty grand, cash. And that is my tit buddy price."

"What do you charge your enemies?"

"Look under there." He kneeled down, pointing a flashlight at the undercarriage. "That's a custom suspension, she'll take a hairpin at seventy without a hint of body roll. And those Brembos? Stop on a frickin' dime and give you nine cents change."

"I don't doubt the quality, it's the price got me choking," I told him.

"Did I mention it has two separate cargo hides, Kevlar door panels? This bitch is a smuggler's wet dream, she makes the Dukes of Hazzard's General Lee look like a pussy wagon."

"I'm sold. Now who am I going to have to fuck to get you to let me have it for a week?"

"If I let you take it for a week, I'm the one getting fucked and I don't swing that way."

"How's a grand sound, and you keep the Crown Vic for collateral?" I offered.

He walked away, kicking up a small cloud of dirt. "Fuck it Moses, I know I owe you, but shit, you're taking bread out of my baby's mouth."

"You don't have any kids."

"Yeah, but I could," he said. "Alright, two grand, and if you dump it you owe me forty, plus I keep the Crown Vic for my trouble."

I reached out my hand. "I could shout rape, but with our history, people might think it was my fault for stepping into your room."

"Bitch and moan all you want, you know it's a sweet deal."

Hitting the gas, I knew he was right, the Scout leapt forward with enough force to pin me to the seat. Jason had done what he could to quiet the 454 down to a subtle roar, at idle it almost sounded like any other SUV, but when the hammer was dropped, there was no mistaking the deep throated rumble of the monster rat. I stowed my weapons in the cleverly disguised lockbox built into the rear quarter panel, all except my snub nose: it, I slipped into the pocket of my leather.

Peter Brixon was waiting in front of his condo, it was one of those classy new buildings in downtown. It had a sign that said if you lived here you'd be home now, plastered so that the slobs stuck in the 101's constant traffic jam could see it and wish they could afford to live there. He had a canvas shoulder tote and a leather briefcase that had seen its better days somewhere in the 1990s.

"Nice car." Peter looked over the Scout, unimpressed. "You want me to drive? I have a BMW 540."

"Of course you do," I said, holding the door for him to get in.

"I just meant, are you sure this thing will make it to Mexico?"

"Yup," I said, climbing behind the wheel. It would have been easy enough to tell him about the Scout, but for some perverse reason, I liked the nervous look on his face.

I had decided not to tell Gregor or Anya I was leaving. Chances were, they would have convinced me to take one or both of them. Anya didn't have the docs needed to cross freely into Mexico, and Gregor was mistaken for an Arab enough to draw heat from the border patrol. That was what I told myself, but maybe it was looking in that window and seeing how normal and happy she looked that made me want to protect her from the jug fuck I was headed for.

It was late enough that the freeways out of town were moving with what we Angelinos had come to call fast: 65 mph with only slight congestion. As I watched the glittering high rises of downtown fade in my rearview, I got Peter to fill me in on the modern slave trade. Since the fall of Communism, Russia's number one export had become women. He rattled off figures and stats like a machine gunner trying to stop the last wave. But the gist I got was that it was international big business, with no end in sight.

"And here, this is the saddest part, we are the end user of all this pain and we don't even know it," he rapped on. "If Johnny mid-level executive knew he was supporting rape, torture and destruction, do you think he would still pay for sex?"

"Absolutely," I said, without a doubt.

"No, if he knew, I mean really got the price these girls were paying for his fun, he wouldn't do it. Not the sickos, they fuck for pain, but Johnny normal, he would stop."

"If you say so."

The Scout proved to be a grand road cruiser, smooth and responsive. After Peter had talked himself dry, he leaned back and was snoring. Around midnight we passed Camp Pendleton, the Marine Corps base where I had done basic before being shipped to that gang bang in the streets of Beirut. Unlike some Semper Fi freaks, it held no warm memories for me. The Marines had taught me to pull a trigger without thinking and not ever trust the old bastards who are giving orders. Fuck questioning authority, there was no question involved, if they asked you to do it, it was a bad idea. If it was a good idea, they'd do it themselves. If what we were doing in that mess was so noble and right, why hadn't I met even one politician's son on the firing line? And here we were stuck in the sand pile again, young men dying with no end in sight. Just thinking about it made my throat dry. It was nothing a good shot of scotch wouldn't cure.

I almost pulled off in San Diego for a half pint, but I knew that would never be enough. Flipping the radio around the dial, I filled the car with classic rock, at least that's what they called it. After sitting through some Foreigner 80s hair band bullshit, Elvis Costello started singing about Alison. By the time she was dragging her fingers through the wedding cake, my mind was filled with Anya. Why the fuck hadn't I taken her to bed when she offered? Instead, I had stuffed my feelings for her down into my gut and pretended I didn't care. I tossed her at Gregor. Were they fucking on his mother's couch while I was on a suicide run south of the border? Bullshit. She was a good woman and he was a true friend. I needed a drink. I needed to get laid. I need the love of a strong woman. But none of that was in the cards I'd dealt myself. Instead, I was stuck on the road with a motormouth reporter looking for trouble that any sane man would run away from.

"What the hell is that?" Peter asked. We were pulled onto a dark street a few miles from the border and I was putting my snub nose into the hidden lockbox.

"A thirty-eight," I said.

"I know that, the other stuff in there?" He was pointing at my Mossberg, a Ruger Mini-14, two Chinese grenades Gregor had found for me, and my 1911.

"You want me to drop you at the bus station?" I asked him.

"No," he said, after thinking about it long enough for me to wonder if he was going to come after all. "You know the Mexican government treats firearms harsher than heroin? We get caught, it will be decades before either of us breathes free air."

"That's why it's hidden."

The pedestrian bridge crossing from Mexico into the States was awash in a flood of drunken college kids and service boys heading home after their night's debauchery. Like smart little gringos they had all parked their cars in the States and taken cabs into Sin City. Apparently they weren't afraid of the cartels, the clap or jail, but if they got a dent in the family car, their dads would kill them. We drove under the bridge and through the border without any trouble. Getting into Mexico had never been the trick, it was getting out that often led to ugly phrases like cavity search.

Skirting downtown and dodging whizzing taxis, I arced through a roundabout and headed toward Playa Tijuana and the Ensenada highway beyond. Tijuana is the sort of town you shouldn't even slow down in unless you are on the bad side of a mean drunk and need to get your ass kicked. I had misspent too many lusty, lonely nights in La Zona Norte when I was stationed at Camp Pendleton. At sixteen, it looked like Oz the first time I crossed that bridge, but that dreamy view turned ugly when it was confronted with the reality of those streets. Woozy, blurred out visions of naked girls I humped and the sweaty pimps I paid are collected someplace in my memory, along with so many others I'm not proud of. These are the photos I pull out at four in the morning to remind myself I really am a sack of shit.

The moon brightly lit our path as we broke free of the city and onto the open coast highway. In the years since I had last traveled this road, it had transformed from a potholed two-lane mess into a modern highway with banked curves and tall cement tollbooths. Dropping a buck twenty into a sweet faced young guard's hand, I accepted his "Buenas noches" and rolled on. Fifty feet from the shoulder, the earth fell away, down steep cliffs lay the restless sea. Waves smashed on the rocks. With the windows open, the air was fresh and salty, with a hint of wood smoke and the rich odor of decay that let me know I was in Mexico.

Rosarito came and went as we powered on. Peter asked if we could stop for dinner, but I wasn't taking my foot off the pedal until we hit Ensenada. Only then, with sixty miles between me and TJ, would I feel safe from her moaning call.

"Ensenada was built in the twenties by Al Capone. Not actually built, but up until prohibition, it had been a sleepy fishing village." Peter was chattering on as we drifted over the hills and down into the small valley that held the town. "He opened a hotel and gambling house, for a few years it was the place for Hollywood royalty."

Ensenada sat at the center of a small bay dotted with fishing boats and pleasure yachts. On a small steep hill to the north of town, large homes perched looking down on the tawdry street life below. It took about twenty minutes of cruising to find the right neighborhood for my particular mission. Past the partying kids at Papas and Beer, past the tourists pressed into Husongs, past the spa resort hotels. On Calle Arande I spotted three strip clubs in a two-block stretch. I was home.

Any doubt was erased when I stepped into the office of Motel 49. The price list on the wall listed $10 for a half-hour, $20 for an hour and $27 for anyone foolish enough to want to spend the whole night. We got two rooms on the upper floor and paid the extra two bucks for a set of towels.

The first thing I noticed about the room was that the door had no deadbolt, not even a flimsy chain, and the doorknob lock could be popped with a butter knife or a good yank. The only window at the rear was a slit in the bathroom, too small for escape. Pushing the dresser against the door, I stripped down and took a shower. It was two AM and the day was starting to wear on me. I told Peter he was on his own finding food and we would hook up in the morning. If I had to listen to his endless patter one more minute, I might have to kill him.

"You want some bud? Crank? I got some pure fucking rock." The kid's accent and choice of dress was straight out of East LA: chinos, plaid shirt over a white tee and buttoned only at the top. He was maybe twenty, but a hard life had given him much older eyes. His hair was cut within a millimeter of bald. Dark prison ink letters S G V scrawled across the back of his skull.

"I don't do that shit since I got out of the joint," I lied, wanting to make it clear I wasn't a tourist pussy he should even think about running his scams on.

"Cool, living above the influence, right? So what you want? You want a titty show? I can take you to the best in town, no bullshit, I'm a Christian so I can't lie." Three other young men his same age and type leaned against a closed taco stand, watching us and scanning for their next customer. These guys were the street version of a concierge. If you needed anything from heroin to a face lift, they could hook you up for a small tip.

"Not into tits? Want a little strange, I got this chick with a dick'll blow your mind and everything else. What'd ya say, you ready to party, muchacho?"

"You ever run into any Russian bitches?" I asked, as casually as possible.

"You mean like from Russia?" His eyes darted away just long enough to tell me he was dodging the question.

"Yeah," I said, smoothing myself back into street hustler mode. "We got some of those Eastern Block bitches up in LA, suck a golf ball through a garden hose."

"They teach them good over there, yeah?" he said, back into his easy sales pitch. "You want a BJ, I gots a bitch with tits out to here, let you come on 'em if you like. Twenty bucks, thirty if you want her top off."

"Slow up ace, just hit town. I wanna look around a bit before I get my knob polished."

"Then come on, I know what you need to see." Taking my elbow, he led me down the block and through the curtain into Le Paris.

It doesn't matter where you travel, a strip joint is a strip joint. A naked little Latina spun on the pole on stage, drunken men sat at the rail staring up at her with glassy, transfixed eyes. The tip boy pushed me down into a chair at a small café table, then went to get me a girl and a drink. Five minutes after hitting the door, I had a barely dressed, barely legal gal on my lap, a scotch in hand and I was only twenty bucks lighter.

"You want to fuck her, they have a back room, safe, I'll wait at the door make sure it all goes down clean," he said.

"I got it from here." I slipped him a ten spot and told him to blow. Pocketing the cash, he faded into the dark club and was gone.

"You want to buy me a drink?" The girl asked.

Who was I to refuse her impossibly large brown eyes? A bar woman with massive cleavage and one wandering eye brought a tequila sunrise, it cost ten bucks and I saw her pass the girl on my lap several pesos.

"I'm Lucy," she told me, pointing out a gold necklace with her name written in cursive. "Just Lucy, not like these indio girls, they have two, three, even four names." Her English was heavily accented but good, even if her grasp of the Spanish origins of multi naming wasn't.

Pulling my arms around her, she told me how much she liked big men, they made her feel protected and comfortable. Downing her drink in three deep gulps, she held it up, shaking it for the bar woman to see. "You don't mind?" she asked me as an afterthought.

Forty bucks later, she was well on the way to sloppy. My scotch sat on the table calling for me to drink it. The amber glow was so inviting. Just one sip, it called to me. To forget the booze, I tried to concentrate on Lucy's voice. She gave me the bar Cliff Notes version of her life, single mother, born in Monterey, her mother looked after her daughter while she worked. She was too young to marry, and no, she hadn't heard of or seen any Russians living in Ensenada. She had dated a German tourist for one weekend, gave her two hundred bucks and a case of the crabs. When the mood hit her, she would grab my face and kiss my cheek, or grind her butt against my crotch, but her attention was too unfocused to get my blood flowing, that and the fact she was a kid, and I'm many things, but a pedophile ain't one of them.

Across the club I watched a sunburned American dance with a squat Indian girl. The music in the room was Spanish techno, but he was moving slow to some ballad in his head. The girl parted his swordfish print Hawaiian shirt, running her hands over his swollen pink belly. After two more drunken turns around the dance floor, she led him into the back. He was done and stumbling out of the club ten minutes later. His grin looked more befuddled than victorious.

Lucy caught me watching the drunk. "You want to go in back? I fuck you good. You like fucking?"

"I think I'll take a pass."

"Whatever." Her head leaned on my shoulder, tequila filled eyes fluttered. At three thirty, they flashed the house lights to let the drinkers know it was last call. I slipped Lucy off my lap, and after a kiss on the cheek I was gone. The streets were mostly empty as I walked back towards Motel 49.

"How was she, did she fuck you good?" My tip boy materialized at my side. "I told you she was primo gash, didn't I?"

"Yeah, she was primo."

"Primo enough for another tip?" he asked, with a Cheshire cat grin that showed off three gold teeth.

"Do I look like your ready-teller?" I let my eyes go cold.

"Shit easy, I'm just fucking with you, homey. So where you staying?"

"Baja Queen." I didn't want him or anyone else knowing too many details. After a long conversation where he tried to sell me everything including his virgin mother, I finally shook him off by promising to hook up with him the next afternoon. We had a street appointment for five PM, we both knew we would be there only if a better offer didn't come up first.

CHAPTER 10

"They found the tarot de Muerte card on the body of one of my best earners two nights ago," Santiago said. He was a tall, aristocratic gentleman in his early fifties, his silver-flecked hair tied back in a shining ponytail.

"This ghost with the tarot cards is an old woman's tale." Kolya stopped pacing and gave Santiago a cold stare. These fucking Mexicans were worse than gypsies, with their superstitions and fucking saints.

"This old woman's tale gutted Gaspar like a fucking fish."

"Stop whining, people die all the time. What does this have to do with me?"

"Everyone knows he hunts for Russian blood," Santiago said, trying to regain control of his emotions.

"Bring it on. I'll show this killer of pimps how we handle punks in my house."

"Bold. Do you want me to write that on your

tombstone?" Santiago felt his old arrogance returning. To hell with the Russian, if he was too ignorant to see a scorpion in his boot, then he deserved the bite. The tarot de Muerte killer was bad for business, his pimps and their minions had refused to work until the killer's head was on a stake. His best men had their ears to the ground. Sooner or later he would find him, and if this Russian son of a whore couldn't be warned, then Santiago would use him like a tethered lamb when hunting mountain lions.

The barking and snarling dog woke Nika from her drifting state, she heard the sound of a car arriving and then a short time later, leaving. What time or even what day was lost to her as she lay in the dark. She still hadn't eaten. How many days? The night the other girls had been taken to meet the men, they had returned late, none had spoken, their eyes were dull and distant. Svetlana brought them a large bowl of warm water and then locked them in; she hadn't even looked at Nika. One by one they washed themselves silently. Nika noticed the water growing pink as Yumma scrubbed between her legs.

After sitting on her bunk and lighting a cigarette from a new pack, Yumma looked at Nika. "If you have to starve to death, don't leave this room."

"What did they do to you?"

Yumma didn't answer. Instead, she lay back and blew a thin stream of blue smoke toward the ceiling.

Later in the dark, Nika could hear Guzel, the girl from Norilsk, snoring and whimpering. When they finally dragged her in she was covered in cuts and bruises. Her nose had been badly broken and was swollen and caked with blood. Nika had cleaned her up the best she could, cooing to her like she imagined a good mother would. The next afternoon, when Svetlana told the girls more men had come and it was time for them to earn their meal, all the young women lined up, heads down, eyes on the floor. Guzel stood on trembling legs and joined them. They reminded Nika of zombies.

"Well, my little princess," Svetlana said to Nika, "are you ready to eat?"

Nika rolled away from the older woman whom she had thought for one foolish moment might be her savior.

Alone in the dark, Nika realized her hunger had faded and was replaced by a deep emptiness. Her strength was all but gone, she could feel herself growing lighter as every moment passed. Soon she would float up off the bed and drift past this hell into the clouds above.

Sunlight was burning through the thin stained curtain when I woke. It was early, too early. I had only been asleep for four hours. Morning wood was creating a tent out of my sheets. Anya's face rolled across my mind. When this was over and I had returned her sister to her waiting arms, then, then I would take her someplace nice, quiet, away from the city. There I would tell her all I was and all I could be with a good woman. What was Anya doing at that moment... still sleeping? Was she alone or had Gregor joined her in the night? I got up quickly and took a cold shower before I let my mind turn me against my young Armenian friend.

Pounding my fist on the door, I roused Peter. He was groggy, and tattered like he had gotten less sleep than me.

"Moses, what time is it?" He was holding the door open only a small crack.

"Time to rock-n-roll, let me in," I said, pushing on the door, but he held it fast, "What, you got a woman in there?" His sheepish grin told me I had stumbled onto the truth. I pushed past him easily. On the bed, a naked young woman was deep in slumberland. I looked from Peter's dipshit grin to the girl and shook my head sadly.

"What the fuck, huh?" he said.

"I'm going for some huevos rancheros. When I get back, have her gone and be ready to work." It was then that I noticed the mirror with telltale white dust and a credit card. "How fucking stupid are you, huh, Pete? Tell me."

"What? So I did a little blow, big deal."

I walked out before I did something irreversible. I wasn't his father or his priest or even his friend. He was a tool and if he didn't work out, I'd drop him in a second.

At a small family restaurant, I got a steaming pile of eggs, pinto beans and fresh salsa served on top of fried homemade tortillas. It filled the hole in my gut and only cost three bucks. Two strong cups of rich black coffee later, I was calm enough to face Peter.

"This is the only way I know to get a story, total immersion." Peter was drinking the cup of coffee I brought him. He was dressed and the girl had vanished.

"Total immersion? Is that what we're calling it now? How old was she? I'm guessing sixteen."

"Fuck off, she was nineteen."

"And you're what, forty?"

"Thirty-eight. What's your point?"

"If you don't get it, I can't explain it."

"You sanctimonious son of a bitch, I bet you're just pissed that I got laid and you didn't." He shot me a smug little smile.

"Did this deep research uncover any news?" I asked, not expecting much.

"I found out Anthony's is a legal brothel slash dance club. You buy a drink, pick a girl, and if you want to take her out, you pay the house a twenty dollar bar fine," he rattled off like a Dictaphone spitting back the facts. "Most of the working girls in town either work out of there or have in the past. None that I talked to have seen any Russian girls working. But after a few lines and half a bottle of Herradura Anejo, the girl you found in my bed let slip that she had heard of a house on the other side of Gringo Hills that is owned by a group of Russians. She didn't know what they do, but the rumor is they're criminally connected to the Santiago family, Baja Cali's numero uno pimp crew. That's about it, but then again, I started late. What did you find out?"

Damn, he was good. I was glad I'd decided not to kill him earlier.

We spent the day driving around Ensenada, getting a feel for the neighborhoods. Gringo Hills was set into the steep mountains to the north of town. Large homes dotted the cliff line, with panoramic views of the bay and the city below. On the flat top of the mountain was a gated community, complete with razor wire-lined eight-foot walls and armed guards to keep out the riffraff. It was the perfect getaway for gringos who wanted a Mexican experience without all those damn Mexicans ruining it. A paunch-bellied uniform watched me roll past the main gate, behind his mirrored glasses, I'm sure he was thinking a truck like mine shouldn't even think of entering unless it was by the service gate. The whole deal reminded me of our compound in the Root. Up until that truck crashed our gate and blew up the barracks, we thought barbed wire and a few guys with M16s could keep us safe. We learned a hard lesson that day: no wall is big enough to protect you from the man who doesn't give a fuck about the outcome.

"Hitler, si, verdad. My mother named me Hitler."

"Your mother didn't name you Hitler." I was leaning against the wall in front of Anthony's, talking to the door man. He was about my age, not as big, but still I doubted many men didn't listen when he talked. He was built solid, his worn suit coat bulged tightly against his muscular forearms. A small pot belly hung over his silver cowboy belt, but that just meant he liked his burritos or maybe cerveza.

"She did. Adolpho," he said.

"That's a good name."

"Si, but to you, Inglés, it is?"

"Adolph, I guess."

"Si, Hitler, no? Adolpho, Jose. Asesino on this shoulder, santo on the other. All night they fight for my soul."

It was mid-afternoon, Peter had gone back to his room

to catch a few winks before our nocturnal hunting. I decided to blow off my meeting with the tip boy. Ensenada was small enough, or at least the tourist area was, if I needed him again it wouldn't be hard to find the little scammer. Anthony's opened at four and stayed that way until four AM or the last of the gringo dollars stopped flowing.

I passed Adolpho a pint of brandy from my jacket pocket. After checking to be sure his boss wasn't in sight, he took a long pull and passed it back. Using my tongue to close off the flow, I mimicked drinking. It would have been so easy to let the warm liquor pour in, who would know? Who, except me and maybe the girl I was looking for, if I got back in the jug and fucked this gig up.

Playing it casual, I chatted Adolpho up, told him I was a bouncer in the States. We shared stories of our lives babysitting beautiful women. He told me he drove a cab when he wasn't at Anthony's. Like most honest working men, it took two and three jobs to keep a roof over his family. He didn't share with his wife the nature of the club's real business. "Wives, they don't understand a man getting paid to watch pretty women all night," he told me.

"I wouldn't know, I was only married for a short time. And she never understood anything about me."

"They are not in la vida to understand us. They are here to give reason for working and a safe place to retirada when the war gets too malo."

"I wish someone had told her or me that, would have saved a lot of cash." Truth was, my home with Jen was a battlefield, not a sanctuary. She had married me to piss off her blue blood father, but when the reality of living with a drunk hood got too real, she checked out and ran back to the

Westside. Last I heard she was engaged to an agent at ICM, and more power to her. I wished the gold plated bitch all the happiness she deserved.

I stood back while Adolpho hurried to the curb to help a stunning woman in a scoop-necked evening gown out of a car. He bent his head, watching her fine ass wiggle into the club, "Calabazo, mango de manila."

"Forget about it," I let out a long sigh. "You ever get to sample the produce?"

"Once, when it was muy lento, storm kept the gringos away, they had a fiesta. Puta on the house. Oye, but only that once."

We watched a silver haired American go in and ten minutes later walk out with a lovely Lola on his arm. They went around the corner and into Motel 49. "Bit long in the tooth to be getting his diver dunked, isn't he?"

"No, señor, see?" He pointed across the street to a farmacia, in its window was a large bright sign happily advertising Viagra and US made condoms.

"Viagra has been good for business?"

"Chingalo! Best invention since pussy, no? One old hombre, he fuck five girls one night, verdad, by the end he no could walk so good, but his miembrillo is muy fuerte." He pumped his fist in the universal sign for a woody.

Tipping the pint up, he drained the last of my hooch. "You ever see any Russians around here?"

"Si, Russians, Germans, a few French, come from the cruise ships. Mostly Americanos. Why you want to know?"

"Truth?"

"Si, truth."

"I'm looking for a girl." I knew he might sell me to the Russians. I had no reason to trust he wouldn't, but I did. "A Russian girl, thirteen."

Adolpho shook his head sadly, "Is no good, niña, she is in Ensenada?"

"I think so," I said. He struck a match and flamed a cigarette. Looking past me to the traffic rolling by, he mulled over this news.

"Ok," he turned his tired eyes on me, "these Russian cabrones, you don't want to fuck with them, but you must, si?"

"Looks like it."

"You know they probably cut out your guts, feed them to the pigs?"

"I think they'll try."

"They don't try. They do. This girl, she is tu familia?"

"No."

"And still?"

"She's in trouble."

"Si, big trouble," he wiped his brow with a white handkerchief. He didn't know exactly where they lived but he had seen them driving around town in big black cars. Once or twice they had come to the club to drink and fuck. Whenever they came, they brought young strapped men who stood by the door and watched them. One of the girls told Adolpho that the older man had his bodyguard in the room while he was getting laid. When he was spent, he gave the girl to the guard. She said they were both rough riders and paid her an extra fifty not to wear condoms. They had laughed saying that they were stronger than any disease.

"I will ask, quietly, see if anyone knows how to find them," he said, "but you be careful. They have eyes on the street." He shook my hand strongly as we parted.

The wings of the pelican burned orange and golden in the dying rays of the sun as it descended into the Pacific. Fishing boats and pleasure crafts bobbed at their moorings in the calm bay. Hard to believe two hundred feet away, some geezer was getting his dick sucked by a chica who was just trying to knock out the rent with the only swag she had to barter.

I walked through the lengthening shadows toward Motel 49. Pushing the dresser against the door, I dropped onto the bed. Closing my eyes, I tried to figure my next move. Somewhere, not far from where I lay, a baby girl was in desperate straits and I didn't feel any closer to finding her. Maybe I had been looking at the problem from the wrong side. I was acting like a John, looking for tail, but these cats had their own supply of gash. If I was them, what would I need?

CHAPTER 11

In the gentle dusk light, a dust crusted Toyota Land Cruiser sat hidden amongst a bramble of manzanitas and scrub oak. Xlmen powered down the windows so that he could better hear the world around. Reclining the truck's seat all the way back, he stretched out. He was a small man even by Mexican standards, but had none of the twitchiness that accompanied so many wiry men. He was at peace in his sinewy body. Tilting his sweat stained fedora down over his eyes, he let his lids drift shut. Waiting was never difficult for the killer. Either in a four by six foot cell or hunting in the mountains of Sonora, waiting was not different. When there was no action to take, he took no action. It was that simple.

Xlmen was Santiago's finest hunter. Sure, he was a sadist and crude in his personal habits, but when it came to making problems disappear, he had no equal. He would have Xlmen watch the hacienda.

Earlier in the day, Santiago dropped a burlap sack on the table between them. Lifting the cloth he exposed the decaying

severed head of Gaspar, Xlmen's cousin. Xlmen didn't blink.
He looked from the head up to Santiago's eyes. "Who?"

Santiago lay the blood stained tarot card on the table.

"Gaspar was family. I want the kill."

"You have earned that right."

Xlmen killed his first human when he was ten years old.
The boy was much bigger than Xlmen's stunted size, he was also
richer. Xlmen knew this because the boy had new boots, a
backpack and Levi jeans. With a primitive garrote made from
baling wire and two short pieces of a broomstick, Xlmen had
strangled the boy. His only feeling at the time was disgust that
the boy had soiled himself and rendered the jeans unwearable.
A mountain lion felt no guilt when a goat stumbled across his
path, why should Xlmen? Life was an endless food chain, and
Xlmen stood at the top. Who knew how many men or beasts
he had dropped in the fifty years after that first boy, who cared?
He took no pride nor had shame in any of it. It just was. And
now the tarot killer had entered his sights. It would only end
one way.

From where he was hidden, he could see up the slope to
the Russian's hacienda, he could also watch the only road
leading in or out. He was comfortable in the deep leather seat
of the luxury SUV Santiago had bought him. He respected
Santiago, he was a man of his word, and he understood how life
worked. The strong fed off the weak. Xlmen had no illusions
about his patrón, if Xlmen grew soft or failed, Santiago would
have him killed. And Xlmen would kill Santiago if he failed to
keep his word, or grew ineffectual.

On the passenger seat sat a satellite phone. If it rang it
would be Santiago, no others had the number. Beside the

phone was a Ruger Redhawk .44 Magnum with a six-inch barrel. Years in a holster had worn some of the blueing off, but it shot true. In the cargo compartment was his scoped Remington 700 hunting rifle and a cut down 12 gauge. Xlmen had no worry about being arrested on weapons charges, Santiago owned policemen, judges and even one mayor. He had procured Xlmen a license as a guide and professional hunter, even the army would let him pass without trouble.

Through his network of pimps and putos, street kids and business men, Santiago had Baja wired up tight. Sooner or later, the tarot killer would surface. Then the satellite phone would ring and Xlmen would go to work.

Gregor's mother spoke very little English. After lots of stumbling, she finally handed the phone to my friend. He told me Uncle Manny had left several messages on his cell asking Gregor to call the club.

"Manny's just sweating because he's down two bouncers," I told him. Doc, the third bouncer, had an expensive girl and two kids with an ex so I knew he could always use the extra shifts. Truth was, Manny was probably worried about us and wanted an update.

"I rolled past my crib," Gregor said. "That King Kong jumbo Ruski had the place staked out."

"He spot you?"

"What do you think?"

"I think you're a fucking ghost when you want to be." I filled him in on what little I had found out south of the border and then had him put Anya on.

"Have you found Nika?" Anya asked as soon as she picked up the phone.

"No, but I'm close." I couldn't stand to tell her the truth, I was miles from anything that looked like close.

"You will find her, you are my strong good man."

"Yeah, that's me."

"You make fun of me?"

"No."

"Yes, but I'm serious. You are a good man."

"If you say so." Getting my mind back on track, I asked her about the Russians who had held her. What did they like, what were their particular vices? I was looking for any handle I could get a grip on.

"Vodka, of course, with every meal many bottles."

"What brand?"

"Vodka is vodka... wait, I remember the old man was yelling at his cook one night because they ran out of Zyr, it is from Moscow, very expensive."

"What else do they like?"

"Russian caviar and, oh yes, those fucking Cuban cigars. Must always be Cuban. Will that help?"

"Yeah, you did good. How is my boy treating you?" It was out of my mouth before I could stop the words.

"Gregor," she hesitated for just a moment and I filled the silence with jealous worry. "He is very good to me, but he isn't you," she whispered the last part, keeping it from Gregor, I was sure.

I dropped twenty dollars on the motel's manager for the phone call and went to wake Peter. At a little after seven, I hoped it was still early enough for him to reach a researcher at the Times. I had him looking for stores that sold Zyr vodka in Ensenada. It was a scarce enough brand, I was betting not many places in Mexico carried it. While Peter worked the phone, I hit the Avenue.

"Prima de Fumar," Teyo, my tip boy, told me. He had explained that if I wanted a bullshit tourist Cuban cigar, I could find them on any corner, but they were crap, some counterfeit Mexican tobacco, others from Cuba but stale from being poorly stored. "No, for the real deal Cuban, Prima de Fumar is the only shop. They closed, but I'll find the owner and I hook you up." Before I could say anything, he had his cell phone out and was rattling away in Spanish. After a rapid fire conversation, he dropped his phone into his pocket.

"We on?" I asked.

"Man, you always in a hurry, you in the land of mañana now."

"Twenty bucks US speed this up?" I dropped a Jackson into his palm.

"You got it, dude, twenty minutes come here and I'll have you smoking one fine cigar." I wasn't sure if he would come through, but this was a fishing expedition and cash was our chum.

Xlmen pushed back his hat, raising the binoculars to his

eyes. A black Mercedes came down the mountain from the hacienda, Xlmen could make out at least three men in the car. He wondered if he should follow them, his orders had been to watch the house, but these men may have been going to find the killer. And if they found the killer, what would they do? They would bring the killer back to their boss. Back up the road Xlmen was watching. Dropping the glasses, he closed his eyes.

The white haired old man in the white room hung up the phone and let out a dry breath. He had kept his temper in check through his entire conversation with the Israelis, but he wondered as he often had if they were worth the trouble. Yes, they inarguably had been a benefit in the growth of his empire, but their constant worrying was like dealing with old ladies, deadly old ladies for sure, but old ladies nonetheless. Now they were panicking over this nightclub bouncer and one girl gone missing. They had given him forty-eight hours to straighten it out, find the bouncer and bring back the woman, breathing or not. It was the insolence of it that galled him most; the implication that he and his men couldn't handle this. Yes, they had failed in the first attempt, but that would not happen twice. Picking up a prepaid cell phone he dialed an equally disposable line in Mexico.

Kolya felt the phone vibrate in his pocket. There were many things he had the power to decide on, but answering his master's call was not one of them. Stepping into the den that had become his office, he locked the door before speaking into the phone, "Dimitri Petravich, I hope all is well with you and Gallina." Gallina was the old man's sour-faced shrew of a wife and although Kolya cared little to nothing for her, not to ask after her wellbeing would be a social misstep that would not be lost on the old man.

"We survive, but are we well? No, Kolya Antonivich, we most definitely are the very antithesis of well." His voice was like two dry sticks being rubbed together.

"I'm sorry to hear this," Kolya said, forcing himself to sound fully subservient, "What can I do to make things better for you?"

"The little package from Moscow, Veronika Kolpacolva, you have her in your possession, yes?"

"Arrived yesterday, with three other fresh ones."

"And how is the training proceeding, no problems?"

"None." Kolya was suddenly worried that someone had told the old man of the trouble the little girl was causing. "They will all be housebroken and eating out of my hand before I ship them north."

"Marvelous, I expect no less from you, Kolya Antonivich, no less and no more." The insult sailed over Kolya's head.

"Thank you, sir, was there anything else you needed?"

"Has there been anyone investigating or inquiring after our Ensenada enterprise?"

"Investigating?" Damn him, how had he heard of this crazy killer Santiago had been whining about? If Santiago had climbed over his head and spoken to the old man, Kolya would have to kill the sleazy greaser. "We own the police, who would investigate us?"

"Possibly no one, but I want you to keep both eyes open

for the time being. Is that crystalline?"

"Sure, I'll spread the word to my men, both eyes open."

"And Kolya, if you lose the little girl, Veronika? It will cost you your skin."

"Sir?" With a click, the connection was cut. Kolya knew this was no idle threat. Years back, when Kolya was still working for the KGB and the old man was a minor gang leader, Dimitri Petravich had skinned a thieving gypsy and nailed his bloody corpse to the door of his wagon. The barbaric act had won the old man his bones with the local mob, and taught Kolya never to cross him.

Flicking on a monitor, Kolya punched up the camera in the girls' dormitory. The girls were all awake, sitting quietly, staring into the unseen distance, all except this Veronika. She lay curled like an infant, clutching her knees to her chest. Her lips were dry and cracked, and what little body fat she had come in with was dissolving away, her small stomach was starting to pooch from distention.

Svetlana had shown him that if they could get the girls to submit willingly, it made them complicit in the act. Their guilt and shame mixed with a healthy dose of fear made them compliant. But Svetlana was wrong about this one, this one would starve before she submitted. And he couldn't have that, not with the old man watching her progress. No, if she didn't come to her senses by the time his men returned from Ensenada, he would have her taken by force. Sometimes all a girl like this needed was a good rough tumble to see the light. It was too bad she wasn't better behaved, if he could have controlled her, she would have brought top dollar from the man who got her cherry.

"Ok, muchacho, it's set," Teyo said.

"Give me the address and I'm gone." I passed him another twenty.

"No, it's close, I'll take you."

"Not necessary."

"These street are dangerous after dark, be a shame for you to get cut up."

"Do I look like the kind of man who gets cut up?"

"No," he let out a nervous laugh, "but the cigar store owner, he knows me, not you, it's close, come on." There was no shaking him, so I had to follow.

We had gone a few blocks when I heard someone calling out my name. Peter pushed his way through the young tourists clogging the street. Teyo didn't look too happy to be joined by a stranger, but he quickly recovered and shook Peter's hand like they were old amigos.

Peter struck out with finding the Vodka, but his researcher would keep on it. It was a long shot, but something might show up in the morning. Turning down a small side street, we walked deeper into Ensenada.

The Americans. One big, dangerous. One small, weak. A stripper told me the big one was looking for Russian whores. I have followed him all day. He is good. Aware. I blend in. Moving deeper into the city we go. My hand is on my blade. Trust no one.

Leaving the tourist district, it wasn't long before we were

the only pale faces. Through a taqueria's grease-streaked window, I saw the place was filled with mariachi. An older man in a dusty black suit sat on the curb plucking out a tune on a large bodied guitarron. A young man sat beside him, watching the older player's hands and trying to follow the melody on his fiddle.

Away from the tourist area street lights were nonexistent. Dense clouds drifted across the moon, blocking out what little light there was. Peter started to look worried as we ventured down darker and poorer streets. "Who the hell would put a cigar shop this far from the main drag? Does this guy think we're complete idiots? Does this look like the kind of place people go to buy fine cigars?" His mouth was in overdrive, while his mind ground gears. Stopping to tie my boots, I nodded for Peter to hold up. The sidewalk under my foot was split with gaping cracks.

I let Teyo get some distance before I spoke. "Shut the fuck up," I hissed, "when this deal blows its main bearing, stay behind me and keep your fucking mouth shut." Shoving my buck knife deeper into the top of my boot, I stood and hurried to catch up with our tip boy.

Stone faced Mexican men watched from the front of a pool hall as we passed. With my hand in the pocket of my jacket, I felt the reassuring diamond cut wood grip of my snubby. A .38 won't stop a bear, but it will make most men think twice about pushing their luck with you. Were we being set up? Oh hell yes, but the only way to find out by who was to let the little punk play out his hand and hope we were holding enough cards to take the pot when he did.

"I knew you'd want to see this." Porfiro, a middle-aged

cop, held several jobs. The first was to protect the gringos who fed the local economy, the second, to protect the locals from the gringos and each other. His third and best paying job was to keep Santiago informed, and his people out of jail. This job allowed his wife to have a nice house on Gringo Hill, not inside the gate, but Gringo Hill nonetheless, it also afforded his daughter college tuition in Mexico City.

He and Santiago were behind a crime scene tape, the flashlight in Porfiro's hand illuminated a blood-soaked body. Red slashes had been sliced up and down and the dead man's clothes hung in tatters. It was as if he had been attacked by a thousand razor-toothed animals. The light's beam rested on the corpse's chest, where a blood spattered tarot card had been placed.

"The last thing I need is this getting out." Santiago knelt and carefully plucked the card from the dead man. "Pimps act afraid and their girls stop obeying, this happens and the order breaks down. Order breaks down and dinero stops flowing. You can see this would be bad for us both?"

"Si claro," Porfiro said. Whatever was happening between Santiago and this pimp killer was none of his concern. It had nothing to do with the people he had sworn to protect. And if by some strange chance Santiago went down, it would be days before another stepped into his place. And the other would need a willing police officer.

The color drained from Peter's face as we turned down a dark alley, his lips were white from the effort to keep from running his mouth. The meager light from the street was left behind, the skinny walkway smelled of piss and rot. Reaching out, I grabbed Teyo from behind, clamping a hand over his mouth, I pressed the .38 up under his chin.

"Squeak, mouse boy, give me an excuse to splatter you," I whispered. He struggled briefly. "Game's over," I pressed the short barrel deeper into his soft flesh. "Who the fuck are you taking us to?" He mumbled into my hand, his wide eyes glittering in the dim light.

"He can't answer with your hand over his mouth," Peter said.

"Did I say you could speak?"

"No, but..."

"Then shut the fuck up, Petey. If I let this boy talk, he's going to lie to me, and then do you know what I'm going to have to do? No? I'll tell you, he lies and I'm going to have to blow the back of his head off. And I'm wearing my favorite jeans. Do you want to clean his brains off them, Petey?"

Peter didn't answer. My guess is at that moment he didn't know who he feared more, this punk street rat or me. "Ok, tip boy," I said, turning my full attention back to my prey, "that day you knew was coming since you squirmed out of your mother's womb is here. You believe in god?"

He moved his head up and down against the revolver.

"That's good, but I doubt you'll be meeting him. You haven't been a good boy, have you? No, you'll be headed the other direction. Now you have one, and only one shot at delaying an early retirement. Would you like not to die?"

Again he nodded.

"Then don't lie to me. One chance, that's it, no do overs, no I'm sorry. Lie and I pop a cap. Got it?" Slowly I lifted my hand from his mouth. As he started to speak, I clamped it back down. "No, the truth." It was an easy guess that he would lie, I had to override any tricky thoughts running in his brain with fear.

"I don't know their name, swear to god," he said when I finally let him speak. "They gave me a hundred dollars to deliver you to them."

"Goodbye." I shoved up on the revolver with sudden force, snapping his head back into the brick alley wall. From the wild look on his face, I was sure he thought he had been shot. When his eyes refocused, all slyness was gone.

"I don't know their names, these Russians, they want whoever has been looking for them. They say they pay big for you. I swear I didn't think they would hurt you, you're my amigo, I not let them hurt you."

"What, you think they may want to ask me to dance? They seem gay to you?"

"They want to talk, that's all, talk."

"Good. Take me to them and we'll talk." I pulled the barrel from his neck and slipped it back into my pocket. "Come on, let's get to it."

CHAPTER 12

We stepped out of the alley into a small courtyard formed by low apartment buildings. A dead oak stood in the center with its leafless branches reaching like skeleton arms into the night sky. No life showed in any of the apartments, the windows broken and boarded over. Trash mixed with discarded furniture and rotting garbage littered the ground.

"Fuck this, man," Peter said, backing toward the alley. "I'm out of here." A stocky man stepped from the shadow of a rusted refrigerator, blocking our exit. At the same moment, two others stood out of the rubble. They surrounded us, even in the dark I could make out the shape of pistols in their hands.

Shoving Teyo to the ground, I dropped and rolled left. The flash and roar of their guns filled the courtyard. But they couldn't see me any better than I saw them. Crawling on my belly, I got twenty feet left of where they had last seen me. Feeling around, I found a discarded beer bottle. Hurling the bottle over my head, I kneeled into a firing stance. The smashing glass was followed by their muzzle flashes. I snapped off two quick shots and dropped down. Someone was yelling painful Russian curses. As I crawled behind a molting sofa, I heard a girlish shriek that I knew could only be Peter.

"Hey dolboy'eb, we have your droog," a voice called out. "Maybe I should cut him?"

"Moses!" Peter was crying like the bitch he was. "He has a knife..." His voice was cut off by a gurgling wet yell. Jumping up, I dove over the sofa, several shots flamed, illuminating a man standing by the trunk of the dead tree. Bullets ripped into the debris around me. I fired three quick shots while running toward the oak.

I didn't need light to know the man was dead. Two of my shots had caught him in the face. Somewhere across the courtyard, the first man I'd shot was moaning. Slipping five new slugs into my .38, I wrist-flicked the cylinder closed and ran at a crouch to the last place I'd seen Peter. To my happy surprise, no bullets followed my movement.

Above us, the clouds moved away from the moon, casting silver light down on the courtyard. Two bodies lay folded onto the ground, both bathed in blood. A dark haired, bearded man I'd never seen before had a slit almost like a second smile cut into his neck. He was quite dead. Peter lay beside him, his eyes glued to the dead man. His lips were trembling but no sound came out.

"You do this?" I asked, sure he hadn't. Peter's eyes slid up at me and tried to focus.

"He's dead," Peter mumbled.

"No shit." A scream of Russian spun me around. Across the courtyard, someone was crouched over a second figure. Whatever was happening didn't sound like much fun for the fellow on the bottom.

Moving toward them, I kept a bead on the crouching figure. Your enemy's enemy isn't always your friend. Getting within ten feet, I could see a slight young man with military cropped blonde hair, he was kneeling on the chest of a wounded Russian. Blood shone on the blade of a straight razor as it arced down, flicking a chunk off the down man's ear. He let out a string of Russian words, but apparently not the ones his captor wanted to hear. Again the blade struck, opening the man's nostril.

I snapped the hammer back on my .38. The sound turned the young man with the blade to face me. He had soft delicate features and cold heartless eyes. He was covered in blood. There was no doubt what had happened to Peter's assailant.

"This is none of your concern. Go home, forget you were here." His voice was higher than I would have guessed.

"Before you fillet this Puke, I need to know where he's holding a friend of mine." I kept the revolver aimed at the lad's head. The bleeding man glanced from the lad to me. He spoke to me in pleading Russian.

"He thinks you can save him," the lad laughed.

"Tell me where the girls are," I yelled at the bleeding man, hoping he understood English. He answered, pleading in Russian.

"What did he say?"

"He wants you to kill me."

"Think he'll take me to my friend if I do?"

"Maybe." His young eyes held no fear.

"Climb off him, slowly." I took a step back, and kept the barrel on his head. Gracefully, the lad rose, wiping the blood off his razor, he slipped it into the pocket of his military coat.

"Where are the girls? Translate." The lad did as told. Russian words flew between them.

"He wants to know if you will let him live if he tells you," the lad told me.

"Talk and I won't kill you, don't and I'll leave now." This brought on an onslaught from the bleeding man. The lad nodded taking it in. In a move so fluid and quick that I barely had time to register it, the youth whipped out the razor, swung down and opened the Russian thug's carotid artery. Dark red spray spewed into the air.

"What the fuck did you do that for?" I yelled at the youth.

"Calle Ruiz, a dirt road twenty meters past the Tecate cut off, they're holding four girls there," he said, slipping the blade away. "That's what you want, isn't it?"

"You didn't need to kill him."

"Yes, I did." He dropped a tarot card onto the man as he bled out, turning the dirt below into red mud.

"Where the fuck are you going?" I asked the lad as he started to fade into the shadows.

"To work."

"Calle Ruiz?"

"Yes."

"You have a car?"

"Not yet."

"You're covered in blood, how far do you think you'll get before someone spots you and calls the cops?"

"I'll be fine."

"Look, whoever the fuck you are, you bailed out my shit here, let me help you get cleaned up. Least I can do."

"And I should trust you, why?"

"You know I'm not working with these punks, and if I wanted to kill you, I'd just pull the trigger and be done with it."

"Fine," the lad said after a long thought.

Teyo had faded sometime during the battle. The little sneak might warn the Russians we were coming, but hopefully his fear had driven him underground until this war blew over. Peter was a trembling mess, but other than his nerves, he was unharmed. The lad dropped a tarot card on the dead man at our feet.

"What's that?" I asked.

"A warning," he said.

"To who?"

"Anyone stupid enough to face me."

Searching Peter's pockets, I found his cell phone. I had a number for Adolpho and hoped I could convince him to take a break and come collect us. Holding the phone up to the light, I discovered there was no signal.

"Fuck fuck fucking fuck we're fucked." Peter was fried.

"No we're not." Moving back through the alley, I noticed how dark it really was. On the street, I scanned for prying eyes and roving gangsters. None appeared.

"Wait here."

"With him?" Peter looked at the silent assassin.

"Yeah." I walked away. At a small bar, I dropped a ten for the use of the phone. The rough boys at the bar sized me up. Wondering if I was worth the trouble of rolling. I'd like to think my street hardened looks kept them off, but truth was I probably didn't look like I had enough on me for them to bother climbing off their bar stools.

Ten minutes later, a late model Toyota pulled up to the mouth of the alley. Adolpho's smile faded when he saw the blood on Peter and the lad. "You want me to take you to médico?"

"The blood's not theirs," I told him.

"So I guess you found your Russians."

"Something like that."

"And this is the niña you were seeking?" He motioned to the lad. I shook my head.

"No, he's the one did most of the cutting."

Adolpho placed an old blanket to protect his back seat and drove us to Hotel 49. Instead of asking me any more questions, he told me about a drunk gringo who had tried to take his son into Anthony's early that night. "He tells me the boy is eighteen, but he looks thirteen, si?" He was grinning, enjoying telling the story. "I say, maybe, but I need to see ID, now the pinche gringo gets enojado, red faced he yell, he is the boy's father and should know his own son's age."

"So did you let him in?" I asked.

"What could I do, he tipped me fifty dollars," he said with a gleeful laugh.

When he pulled up to the hotel, I asked him the fare. "Nada, is por las niñas," he said. I didn't insult him by pressing it. I shook his hand and promised to let him know when we had freed her. He looked like he thought that message might be a long time coming, but he didn't say anything.

The lad tightened when I pushed the dresser against the door. Before I could explain about the lack of a good lock, the razor was out and swinging at my face. I caught the arm inches from lacerating my cheek. A boot shot up and connected square on my nads. I dropped to my knees, fighting to keep the puke down. I rolled onto my side as a second kick sailed past my head. This little punk was fixing to kick my ass.

"What the fuck is your damage?" I yelled, ripping the .38 out of my pocket.

"To take me, it will have to be dead." Again the blade swung up.

"I don't want to do shit to you. Now put the razor down before I forget we're on the same side and blow a hole in your face."

"You want to fuck me. Tell me I'm wrong."

I suddenly started laughing, all the adrenaline and

general bad craziness of the night had hit critical mass. He wasn't a he, he was a she, and she wanted to slice me up out of some Diana driven man hatred. The laughter made my balls hurt worse but I couldn't stop. She looked down like I had gone mad, and maybe she was right.

"Look, as beautiful as you look bathed in blood and all, you just aren't my type." I lowered the .38. "I go for something a little less... deadly in my lady friends." The blade was still hovering up above her head, ready to strike. "Screw it, slit my throat or take a shower, choice is yours."

Rolling over slowly, I crawled on all fours over to the bed and hoisted myself up onto it. When I was able to see the room, she was gone and the bathroom door was shut. She had moved as silent as any cat, she dealt out a mean knife, if it wasn't for her wanting to kill all men, she might just be my type after all.

The worst of the nausea had passed by the time she came out. With the blood gone and lights on, it was clear she was a woman. A thin scar ran from below her left ear to the corner of her lips. Wrapped in a towel it was clear she was missing her right breast. A jagged spider web of scars spread up from the towel and into her neck line. They were all old scars, pale and slightly raised lines of some distant trauma. She had an athlete's build, all muscle and sinew, if she had an ounce of body fat it wasn't apparent.

"My clean clothes are in a locker at the train station," she said.

"And?" I smiled at her stupidly.

"I can't go like this."

"True."

"Do you have anything I can put on?" she said quietly. It was obvious she had difficulty asking for anything, and I wasn't about to make it easier on her.

"So first you make sure I'll never be able to have children, and then you want to borrow my clothes? That about right?"

"You locked me in. What did you expect?"

"Not to get my balls kicked in was on the list, thought maybe you'd get a shower and then tell me what your part in this game is."

"What game?"

"Hide, seek and destroy the Russian mob. Your accent, Russian right?"

"Ukraine." Her arms were across her chest, and her face was free from emotion. I made a note not to ever play poker with her.

"You want these?" I pulled a pair of chinos and a tee shirt from my duffle. She reached for them but I yanked them back. "No, answers first, then clothes."

Setting her jaw, she turned and started to pull the dresser from blocking the door. She was clearly willing to walk out into the streets of Ensenada dressed only in a towel rather than be pushed into answering my question.

"Fuck it." I tossed her the pants and shirt. Without a thank you or even a grunt of gratitude, she slipped into the bathroom and got dressed. Pulling a web belt off her blood stained pants, she cinched up my huge chinos and dropped the razor into her pocket.

"Any chance we can talk like civilized people, without

one of us getting cut to shreds?" I asked with a loose smile.

She leaned against the dresser, keeping a good distance between us.

"If I'm such a dirt bag, why am I risking my life to help some little Russian girl I never met?"

"People lie all the time."

"They sure do. Time to roll the dice and hope I don't come up snake eyes, or walk out the door."

She dug a pack of Mexican smokes out of her coat. Striking a kitchen match, she inhaled a lung full of nasty smelling tobacco. Letting the blue gray smoke roll out over her thin lips, she spoke so softly I had to strain to hear her words, "If you betray me. I will kill you."

"Sounds fair. You going to fill me in on what you're doing down here?"

"No."

"Right. Do you have a name?"

"Mikayla." That was it, no last name. After a few more lame tries, I stopped asking questions that she wouldn't answer.

I was getting my .45 out of the Scout's hidden compartment when Peter joined us. His color was back to pink, and he looked more confident. "You're not coming on this run," I told him.

"Why, because I freaked when a man got his throat slit on top of me?"

"You weren't in Afghanistan or Haiti. Are you even a reporter?" I asked. Mikayla watched Peter suspiciously over the hood of the truck.

"You want to see my press credentials? Is this some macho testosterone power play, big man Moses gets to judge who is man enough to go on his little death trip?"

"I don't roll with liars, or wannabe tough guy cherries. Seen 'em get too many guys killed."

"Screw you. Ok, I never was in those places, I lied, big fucking deal. You take me with you and I'll be fair witness to what goes down. If this shit doesn't get reported in the States, it will keep going, spreading like a malignant tumor. You shut them down, they'll open three more safe houses before you cross the border. Am I using you to further my career? Yes, absolutely. But you can use me to put an end to this sleazy deal."

I was about to tell him to fuck off when Mikayla spoke up, "He comes with us." I wanted to ask her who made her captain of this party ship, but I realized she was right. What good was saving Nika if ten more took her place? The newspapers might also be our only hope if this shit got wicked back in LA. I hadn't a clue why the feds were eyeballing me, but I knew the one thing ol' Unkie Sam was afraid of was bad press.

CHAPTER 13

The streets were jammed with late night party drunk tourists. A toasted little blonde number stumbled out into traffic as we rolled past Papas and Beer, her shirt had come untied in the front and she was flashing more than a little bra.

"Jesus Christ, Judy, maintain!" a boy in Dockers and a polo shirt yelled as he jerked her back, "We are in Mexico, Judy! Maintain!"

The boy's fear of the foreign made me smile. Back in wonderful LA, we had drive-bys, home invasions and a murder rate that might freak residents of Ensenada. All this preppy boy could see was brown skin and Spanish switchblades. What the fuck, he probably lived in Brentwood and had every reason to fear the unknown.

Breaking free of the traffic jam, we pulled onto Highway 1 and headed out of town. Peter was boldly staring at Mikayla. From the white crust faintly dusting the rim of his nostrils, I suspected his courage was supported by the Bolivian troops marching through his veins.

"You're the tarot killer, aren't you?"

Mikayla looked at him, her icy blue eyes bore through his forehead to focus on a spot a hundred yards past the back of his skull.

"Is it true you took out pimps from Tel Aviv to Mexico City to Cancun? Confirm? Deny? What?" The twitchy little fucker was on a coke-fueled roll. "It's her, right?"

"Keep me the fuck out of this. Two hours ago I thought she was a male psycho killer, now I just think she's a psycho killer."

"I know it's you, I heard you're called Madre Muerte. Oh, it's you alright. One story has you coming out of Odessa, it's all very shadowy, covert, vague rumor mill, some say that the Tel Aviv brothel fire was your doing, any comment? Come on, give me something, anything. Rumor has it, you stood in the street gunning down the pimps and their boys as they ran out of the burning building. What do you say about that?"

"I hate guns," she said, turning to look out the window.

"I like her, Moses, a sweet mix of psychotic ice queen, and bull-dyke axe murderer."

"I don't think she cares two shakes of an ant's ass whether you like her or not." Her silence told me I was correct. Ten minutes out of town, we saw signs for Tecate and a small dirt road marker, Calle Ruiz.

A red brown rooster tail of dust spewed from the Scout's rear tires. Bouncing up and over a small rise, the lights of a lone hacienda glowed from a hilltop ahead of us. No other lights showed in the small valley or up on the hill. I killed the headlights and drove by sheer feel, while my eyes adjusted.

"Are you completely nuts?" Peter asked.

"Pretty much, yeah."

"Turn on the lights before you get us killed."

"You afraid to die, Pete?" We bounced over a deep furrow, Peter let out a high girlish squeak. "You want them to see us coming, have time to get ready, maybe lay out a cheese ball, some punch?"

"It won't help them, even if they do." Mikayla was completely sure of herself. She was a zealot on a mission from a very angry god.

Near the foot of the mountain, an iron gate blocked the road. I pulled the Scout into a small gully and set the emergency brake. "We'll hoof it from here." I gave Peter my .38 and strict instructions to stay in the truck. I said if he heard gunfire he was to crash the gate, roar up the hill and get us the fuck out of there.

"Screw that, Moses, you said I'd have full access to the story, I want to be where the action is." Bless his coke-brave heart, I thought not for the last time that I should put one between his eyes and tell god he died.

"Dead men may win a Pulitzer, but they don't have much fun at the awards dinner." His face fell as my words hit him. His inner pussy was battling it out with his chemical bravado. The pussy won. It always does. His eyes darted into the darkness surrounding us.

"You think they'd actually kill me?" His eyes darted into the darkness surrounding us.

"Without hesitation." Slinging the Mini-14 over my

shoulder, I slipped extra clips into my pocket and started up the hill with Mikayla. I heard the truck doors locking behind me. Peter, the poor son of a bitch, thought a locked car door would save him if this deal got wet. Locks only keep honest men out, and I had a feeling whoever was waiting for us up the hill, they were anything but honest.

Xlmen's boots made close to zero noise as he stepped out of his SUV. He had seen the truck roll up the canyon. Even with binoculars, he hadn't been able to spot its inhabitants, but driving with headlights off was a dead giveaway that it wasn't coming for any good reason. From where the truck had disappeared, he plotted a trajectory up the hill. Moving quickly down an animal track, he was careful not to make a sound.

Peter watched Moses and the girl disappear into the scrub, he clutched the .38 in his sweat drenched hand. Was any story worth this? Had he weaseled his way in over his head? A turn of the key and he could be headed back home. Screw McGuire and his psycho dyke girlfriend, the Russians would most likely waste them. On the other hand, if they survived and he rabbited on them, they would kill him. Could they find him? They had found the Russians. How hard would he be to track down?

Opening a small folded envelope, Peter shook a short fat line out. Rolling up a twenty, he snorted. Rubbing the left over powder onto his gums, he felt the reassuring rush. Fuck the Russians, he could handle whatever those Slavic bastards sent his way.

I motioned for Mikayla to follow me as I crept in a circle around the hacienda. It sat on the flattened off top of a small hill, it looked to have been built back in the days when Spain ruled this patch of dirt. Deep windows were cut into the thick adobe and covered with ornate ironwork bars. No guards with guns peered out the windows, apparently they figured a remote location was all the safety they needed. Or perhaps we had killed the lion's share of their men down in Ensenada. The only point of entry was a ten-foot wooden gate that was bolted from the inside.

"Time to divide our eggs," I whispered. "I'm going over the roof. If I don't get nailed I'll open the gate."

"And if you get nailed?"

"Then I'm counting on you to avenge me."

Using the ironwork over a dark window I climbed up onto the red tile roof. The pitch was close to flat, but every step creaked and the old tiles felt ready to crack and give away my position. From the rooms below my feet, I could hear the muffled mumble of conversation; somewhere a radio was playing the dull thump of dance club music. Crawling on hands and knees, I made it to the roof over the front gate; below, an open courtyard held several cars and a white van. Slipping over the edge I was able to lower myself onto the van's roof. I paused, crouching for a long moment, listening for any sign of alarm. The music thumped on and a male voice crooned along with it.

Sliding off the van, I dropped softly to the dirt. A deep growl rumbled behind me. Twisting at the sound, I saw a massive blur of brown fur, muscles and teeth leaping out of the shadows. The pit beast leapt straight at my throat, jerking back, I escaped death by less than an inch. Stumbling with the force of the flying dog, I latched onto his neck as I fell to the ground.

The powerful jaws snapped inches from my face. It took all my strength to hold him off. The steaming scent of rotten flesh from his breath filled my lungs.

Curling my boot up into his belly, I kicked up. The beast flew up and away. It landed ten feet from me, winded, then it was up and charging me again. I pulled my buck knife from my boot, snapping it open as the creature leapt. His eyes went wide as I drove the blade up into his throat. He kept snapping at me, even in the throes of death. Twisting the knife, I rolled over so that I was on top of him. Warm blood soaked my arm and chest. When I thought it was over, he reared up, a twist of my head kept him from ending my life, instead of my throat he sank his canines deep into my shoulder.

Dropping my blade. I grabbed his jaw, as I fought to free myself from his grasp, he let out a long exhale and went limp. His last act had been to try and kill me, I had to respect his devotion to the task.

Looking down at his corpse, I heard something whistling through the air. From the corner of my eye, I caught a glimpse of a shovel as it flew toward my head. The world shattered into a spark filled pain. Then nothing. Black empty nothing.

CHAPTER 14

Pain flared in my shoulder and spread like wildfire across my body until it completely engulfed me. My muscles clenched in a powerful spasm. My back arched and my limbs shot out. My eyelids snapped open. I was unable to focus on or comprehend the room around me. A blurry form reached out and pressed a short stick into the dog bite on my shoulder. Volts of electricity blasted through me, blowing out my circuitry as it roared across every nerve ending. The wave passed, leaving me limp. I could taste the salty iron of blood in my mouth where I had bitten a small chunk out of my tongue.

Somewhere in the blurred fog around me, I heard a man speaking Russian. An ugly pockmarked face leaned in close to my face. "You are who?"

I opened my mouth, to plead, to beg, to cajole, whatever it would take to make the pain stop. But I was betrayed by my gut, instead of words - a nicely chunky spray of vomit spewed.

"Vali otsyuda!" He jammed the cattle prod into my shoulder, but before he could trigger the jolt, he was pulled away by a second form. In the shadows, a guttural Slavic argument bounced off the walls. Focus was returning. Out of the mess, a barn or garage formed around me. I was strapped down on a work bench. On a peg board, power drills, saws and hammers rested, waiting to be put to bad use.

"It's for you." A furry man in a blue satin jogging suit pressed a cell phone to my face.

"Mr. McGuire, you have outlived my expectations." The voice was dry, Russian and void of any human emotion. The old man in the white room. I should have killed him when I had the chance. "However, you have now outrun your expiration date. I now have one last offer to make you, the man whose home you have defiled has asked permission to exact retribution, slow, painful retribution. Apparently, you brought on the early demise of his beloved pet. And here is where the offer comes in, pay close attention. Tell me where I can find Anya and I will command Kolya to execute a swift end to your life." I could hear his breath as he waited for me to reply.

"Suck... my... dick," I mumbled as clearly as I could muster. The fur-ball in satin slapped me across the face. He spoke quickly into the phone, then snapped it closed and sent his pockmarked lackey out of the room.

"If your Armenian is out there, Zhenya will find him." Picking up a rusted hacksaw, Kolya toyed with it. Running his thumb lightly down the blade, he looked me over like a butcher appraising a side of beef. "The boss doesn't think pain will loosen your tongue. Is he correct?"

I had learned in prison to relax my face muscles, regardless of the storm in my head. A neutral face showed no fear. He might kill me but I wasn't about to show him I cared one way or the other.

"I think maybe I will kill two birds with one blunt object." From his pocket he took a small pillbox. "Do you know what is the great motivator? Not fear, no. Guilt. Pain fades and must be re-administered. Guilt can break a person for life." Grabbing my jaw he forced my mouth open. Like you would an animal, he tossed several pills into my mouth, he chased them with a bottle of vodka upended past my lips. Glass smacked against teeth. My throat shut down. Short stubby fingers clamped onto my nostrils, I had to drink or drown.

The quart was halfway down when he pulled it away. Sputtering, I struggled to fill my lungs. The neck of the bottle cut my lip against my teeth as he shoved the bottle back in my mouth. Drink or drown.

Dropping the empty bottle, he looked at me and let out a small laugh. "Think of this as your last meal. Vodka, what more could a man ask for?" I was brain fucked. Searching for some bullshit comeback line. But he was gone. I was alone, me, my fear and whatever pill he gave me. That and the vodka. I wished it didn't feel so good. But it did. That familiar glow, that everything-will-be-fine sensation. I knew it was a whore's promise, but one my body was fighting to accept. Warm cotton candy wrapped itself around my pain and told it to go home, come again some other day. Somewhere in another country, men shouted in Russian. The rusting blade of a jigsaw came in and out of focus.

I am quiet. I wait. I hunt. I watch as the large American drops out of sight. I move around the perimeter. I hear a dog attack. I hear men moving. His problem. Below us a body moves. Only a glimpse. We are being hunted from below. I drop, silent. Hide behind an outcropping. I watch. I wait. Nothing. Someone is coming up from the valley floor. I can feel them. But I am blind to their movements. They are good.

I close my eyes and flare a match to life. I feel my way to light a cigarette. I blow the match out. My eyes need no adjustment. I drop the cigarette. A hundred yards below something shiny twinkles. A rifle sight. It will take him time to find me.

Fuck. I fought to free my arms. Fuck. My heart was starting to race unnaturally fast. I fought to slow my pulse but it was a runaway train. Loopy thoughts crowded for attention. What was her name? The Ukrainian assassin, I could see her cards, but the name?

Thump thump.

Fuck, I was going to die.

Thump thump thump.

Angel, I wanted my dog.

Thump thump thump thump. My fucking heart was pounding like a pile driver. The throbbing in my temples climbed on top of the vodka and reminded me I'd been hit in the head with a shovel.

Time went sideways. Where the fuck had all the sweat come from? Beads rolled off my face, stinging my eyes. The furry little fireplug swam out of the shadows. His pockmarked pal was grinning down at me. Mikayla. That was her name and she hadn't slit his ugly throat. I was well and truly fucked. Someone started laughing, high pitched and sad. It was me.

Nika lay alone in the dark. They had moved her into a small bare room. On the cold tiles, she lay without the comfort of a pillow or blanket. Her self-imposed fast had driven her into a soft madness. She could no longer remember why she had refused to go with the other girls, only that she couldn't give in. She had made her peace with the fact that she would die on this cold floor. Whatever she had hoped or dreamed for in her life was now never going to happen. Oddly, she had come to be ok with this fact. She could see how silly her dream of being a star in America was. She was sorry that she would never see Anya again, but it was how it worked out. Fate had given her thirteen years and that would have to be enough.

A dog choker pinched my throat. Pockmark pushed his pistol into the base of my skull, yanking the chain at the same time. The floor felt rubbery and the walls kept tilting on me. Keep moving. Stumble and this twat will kill you. And thump thump thump my rapid-fire heart. Was I dreaming or did I have a raging erection? No. Not dreaming. It was hurting as it tried to explode the seams of my jeans. What the fuck? Really. What the fuck was happening?

From the hallway outside, she heard footsteps coming towards her, then the key in the large old lock. Light flooded in, hurting her eyes. Looking up, she saw a tall man filling the doorway. The huge man swayed as if he might fall over at any moment. With his wild red-blonde hair and beard, he looked to her like a wounded Viking berserker.

A party dress rag doll lay on the floor. Eyes open, looking up at me. Fawn eyes, caught in the headlights, more animal than human. A wave rolled across the floor, almost toppling me. I grabbed the doorjamb to keep from going down.

"This is what you came for, no?" Kolya's voice traveled from miles away. I could feel his breath on my ear. The rag doll scrabbled away pinning her back against the wall.

"I don't know why you have gone to so much trouble. She refuses to fuck. And what good is a pussy that won't fuck?" The girl pressed her face into the wall. Kolya grabbed a handful of her tangled hair and dragged her to my feet. Tugging her hair back, he forced her face up. This is no rag doll. She is a beautiful child. The sound of her dress ripping exploded like thunder. I wanted to close my eyes, not have her see me leering at her young body. But I couldn't.

"This one, she needs a good fucking, and you, well you look ready to help out." He was looking down at the clear bulge in my jeans. I wasn't a pedophile. I didn't fuck children. But apparently my cock did. I hated the way it felt, blood-filled and ready. Hated that any part of me could want to fuck this child.

The girl looked out at me, her eyes pleading. Bile backed up into my throat, I was close to puking. Even in the face of that, the spinning room and the wanting to puke, the betrayer in my jeans throbbed out a rhythmic pulse. I leaned forward, forcing the chain tight, hoping to choke.

"You don't look happy. Are you a faggot? You take this little bitch, or tell me where the big sister is hiding. Like god, I have given you free choice." The sick bastard was enjoying this. Slowly I shook my head, the room spun slowly with the motion.

Kolya knelt down, a pair of wire cutters in his hand. "You don't care if I hurt you, but what about her?"

"Don't." The choke chain turned my voice into a rasp.

"Don't what? This?" One moment he was reaching for the girl's foot and next she was screaming. Blood rushed from the stub that had been her little toe. He picked up the amputated toe and tossed it carelessly over his shoulder.

I charged in blind rage, but I only took two steps before the chain ripped me back. My feet skittered out from under me and I went down. Pockmark pinned me under his boot, pressing my face to the floor with a revolver barrel. Kolya wrapped a handkerchief around the squirming girl's stump. Grabbing a fresh toe, he looked over at me, "I hope you will be a man before I get to her fingers."

"Stop. I know where Anya is..."

"No!" Nika yelled through her tears. "Please. Don't. Look at me. We are dead. Don't kill my sister too. I want you to have me. Not one of these fat pigs." Cries became whimpers, "Please take me... I want you... please..." She reached a hand toward me, pleading. Kolya released her foot, he had finally broken her. He looked down at her with pride in a job well done.

"Then it's decided," he said. "She wants you to have her precious cherry, to save her whore sister. How fucking sweet, no?"

Nika's eyes locked on mine, they begged me to do this thing. I was a dead man. But if they saw her comply, she would live. Dead whores earn no cash. That was the only hope I could find in this ugly mess.

"Bring him," Kolya snapped. Pockmark walked me, crawling like a dog on a tight leash until I was almost on top of the girl.

Something has gone wrong in the hacienda. A man, a

157

flashlight, searches from above. A light beam cuts through the surrounding brush. It's been thirty-four minutes since they took the big American. I doubt he is still alive. The hunter from below still stalks my moves. I have doubled back twice and not lost or caught him. Whoever he is, he is good enough to kill me. Dead, I do no good. Trapped between the two. I crawl up the hill. I stay on my belly. I move towards the moving light. He is overweight. He has a child's face. He has a machine pistol in his hand. When he turns away from me, I move. Springing out, I stand. I swing the razor. He turns. Instead of jugular I slice chunk of neck meat, severing his tendon. His head flops to the left. He lets out a scream. I swing again. He uses the gun as a shield, blocking the blade. My left hand pulls the hunting knife from my belt. I bury it in his back. His scream becomes a death wail. He drops the gun. The razor slices through his throat, quieting his scream to a gurgle.

Somewhere beyond the walls I hear an inhuman scream. "No rescue coming. That will be your boy dying. Now get to the fucking before I get bored and shoot you both."

Fumbling, I unzipped my pants. My eyes stayed locked on the girl's. She opened her legs as I climbed on top of her. Her eyes dilated when she felt the tip of my penis brush against her pubic hair. Pockmark had his boot on my ass, and he was starting to laugh and chatter in Russian. I wanted to tell her nothing real could ever be taken from her. But I know that was a lie. Pockmark pushed down, forcing me into her. The girl let out a stifled cry. As I felt myself entering this dry unprepared child, something snapped deep inside my soul.

Driving my fist down, I arched my back and swung up. The motion knocked the boot off me, as Pockmark stumbled I grabbed the chain around my neck and yanked him toward me.

Rolling to the left, I pulled him down onto me. His pistol clattered from his hand. Grabbing his ears, I twisted and turned over, landing on top of him. With his ears firmly held, I drove his head down onto the cold tiles. He screamed. I screamed. I slammed his head down again, his skull made a sickening wet crunch. I couldn't stop. Down went his head, he stopped screaming. His body twitched wildly. Blood and brains slopped from his skull as I continued to pound him into the floor. Somewhere in a distant world, I heard a gun cock. Dropping the ruined man's head, I glanced up. Kolya was aiming a small automatic at my face.

A roar and flash filled the dim room. Kolya looked down, amazed at the blood draining from his chest. The second shot took him in the gut. His face went from surprise to rage. Then the third shot clipped his shoulder. He fell against the wall. Sliding down, he left a slick trail of blood. He looked down at the oozing blood, surprised, the possibility of being shot had never crossed his mind.

"You bitch, who do you think you are?"

Nika answered by emptying the pistol into his chest. He was dead before the gun clicked onto an empty chamber. She kept squeezing the trigger, clicking on spent shells. Taking the gun from her hand, I tossed it away. She didn't see me, she was focused on something much farther than the small room could hold. Lifting the automatic that the dead man had dropped, I pulled the girl to her feet. She swayed weakly, her knees buckled. Slipping my arm under hers, I kept her standing. Adrenaline was doing a fair job of countering the booze. The room was still swimming, but I could navigate it. I closed one eye to keep my vision from doubling up on me.

"Where... are the others?" She looked at me, without comprehension. Her eyes rolled up and she went slack. Lifting her over my good shoulder, I dragged my gun hand along the wall for balance. I pushed into the hall. The house was still, in the living room I laid the girl down on a leather sofa. Slumping down beside her, I wanted to sleep, drift off and wake in my bed with Angel. Like a shark, I knew I had to keep moving or die. I didn't know how many thugs were still alive in the hacienda.

Stumbling from room to room, I opened doors, but found no one waiting to kill me. In the back of the hacienda stood a thick oak door, it was locked, when I rattled the knob I could hear soft voices. Leaning back, I kicked the door, it bowed and cracked but held tight. I bounced backward. Hitting the far wall, I stumbled down onto the tile.

From inside, a girl cried out. Squinting, I pulled the door into focus. A large key jutted from the lock. Dumb fuck. I turned the lock and opened the door. A plump older woman stood in front of three frightened girls, she looked like a tarted up mother hen.

"Kak dala?" The mother hen moved towards me.

"English." I leveled the small pistol at her.

"Kolya will kill you." Her eyes were flaming mad.

"He's dead." Her face dropped its anger as she started to panic.

"Oh, thank god. You have come to save us," she said, her eyes darting around, looking for escape at the same moment she was trying to convince me she was happy about this new turn of events.

From the canyon beyond the house, a large caliber gun rumbled, one, two, three shots, then it was quiet. "Time to roll." I pushed off from the jamb, motioning with the pistol for them to follow.

The mother hen led the girls after me. Picking Nika up off the sofa, her eyes drifted open. She looked around the room with a vacant dreamy gaze. I lifted her up over my shoulder. The floor buckled. I wanted to puke, but kept moving.

Passing through the kitchen, I stepped out into the courtyard. Nika's body went stiff. Something behind us had scared her. I swung around to find the older woman running at me; she had a butcher knife up over her head. I fired without thinking. A small hole appeared between her eyes. She dropped like a sack of round soft rocks. The three girls stepped over her body without even looking down. Apparently none of them would shed a tear for the old bitch.

Headlights bounced up over the front gate and I could hear the throaty rumble of the Scout as it skidded to a stop.

Peter's pupils were pinned. "Who the fuck are they?" he asked, looking at the small tribe of girls following me. Noticing my damage, he let out a small gasp. "What the hell happened to you?"

"Bad things." Setting Nika in the back seat, I almost tumbled in on her. Righting myself I motioned the other girls into the back.

Peter looked at the still rock hard erection outlined in my jeans.

"They fucking doped me - Viagra... let's roll." The ground was pitching causing me to sway.

"You can't drive."

"Fuck you." I slid in behind the wheel, turning the key, I

ground the already running engine. "Where's Mikayla?"

"Not with you?"

"I heard shots."

"There were some flashes near the foot of the mountain, but I didn't stop to check it out or anything. You said if I heard shots I should come to the house and that's exactly what I did." He was speaking so fast, I was amazed he didn't pass out from lack of oxygen. Whoever had been firing was most likely still down there. I mashed the gas pedal, spinning the Scout into a dusty 360; we almost hit the front gate.

"I can't drive." Moving into the passenger seat, I let Peter take the wheel. We caught air flying off the ridge. Slamming down, he fought for control and almost took us off the road. The xenon lit a bright path down the dirt road. Slamming around a rutted curve, we sprayed dirt and rocks out behind us. Hitting the door, my shoulder screamed red pain.

Peter was concentrating like a fiend. Bouncing up over a bump the size of a tree trunk, I flew up, my head thumped up into the roof. I squealed. I didn't ask him to slow down.

Coming off the hill, the valley spread before us. Pounding up out of a small gully I saw a dark figure in the middle of the road.

"STOP." It was almost too late when I realized it was Mikayla. Locking up the brakes, the Scout fishtailed sideways, Peter fought the wheel to keep us from either rolling or hitting Mikayla. When we finally stopped moving, I saw her standing statue still, with dust settling down around her.

"Fuck this." Peter jumped out, kicking dust, screaming into the night, "Fuck this. I didn't sign on for this shit, no way, ask a few questions, get an interview, fine. Not this crap!"

Mikayla leaned in the window, ignoring Peter's rant. Noticing the shaken but free girls in the back she came as close as she was capable of to smiling. Then she looked at my raggedy ass. "You are alive."

"More or less," I said.

"You drunk?"

"As a skunk."

"Interesting choice."

Headlights flared up behind us. Mikayla dove into the driver's seat, dropping the hammer, the truck lurched forward. Peter had to run to keep from being left. He climbed in next to me as we took off.

Our new shadow was coming cross country, angling to meet up with us long before we could make the highway. I silently thanked Jason B for the heavy duty shocks as we flew across ruts deep enough to cripple any soccer mom's SUV. The speedo swept up past sixty. Cactus and brush were brown and green blurs out the side window. In the back, the girls were screaming and crying, they must have thought I pulled them from the frying pan and dropped them smack down in the middle of hell.

Mikayla was pure cold concentration. The chick could drive, I'll give her that. Out of the side window, I could see that we were making ground on the bouncing headlights. If she kept the speed up, we would be well ahead of him before he intersected the dirt track. Gold eyes glowed red in the headlights, a coyote crossed into our path. The small critter was frozen with fear. Mikayla wasn't slowing. I grabbed the wheel and spun us to the left.

I had already killed one dog that day, I didn't think my karma could handle another. Bumping off the road, the windshield filled with brown and green. We hit a barrel cactus with enough force to dent the center of the grille and hood. Steam started to geyser up from the ruptured radiator. Mikayla fought the wheel. We swiped a small manzanita and skidded back onto the road. The steering was pulling hard to the right, she was struggling to keep us on the road. The temp gauge started to climb towards the red line.

We were running out of options, there was no way the damaged Scout would outrun our pursuer. Grabbing the emergency brake, she locked the back tires; yanking the wheel to the right she spun us in a half circle. Releasing the brake she headed away from the highway, back towards the hills.

"What the hell are you doing?" Peter screamed. "The road home is back that way, you crazy…" Whatever else he said was lost in the high pitched whine screeching out of the engine. The temp gauge was locked firmly in the red as 454 cubic inches of blueprinted horsepower started to rip itself apart. The road twisted sharply up, heading back to the hacienda. Foul black smoke joined the steam billowing up over the windshield. Visibility was down to zero. Keeping us on the road was mostly guesswork. The only good news was that I had yet to see any headlights behind us.

Cresting the hill, Mikayla hit the brakes, misjudging by only a few feet. We slammed into the side of the adobe wall. My head bounced down onto the dash. "This fucking night…" I mumbled. Our cargo was well shaken but they all seemed to be able to move.

"There's a van," I slurred at Mikayla as we piled out of

the ruined truck.

"What are you doing?" Peter asked as I pawed at his pocket, coming up with the small envelope.

I didn't answer him.

Nika was moving, but weakly. Mikayla gently put an arm under hers and helped Peter get the girls into the courtyard.

On the Scout's dashboard I dumped out what was left of Peter's coke. Two fat lines brought my eyes back into focus. I rubbed the last of it into my shoulder wound. It burned like a mother when I touched it, but the coke did the job, laying a layer of numb over the ache.

The tranny was fucked, it took three tries to muscle it into reverse. Swinging it around, I aimed down the hill. Out across the valley floor, blurry headlights sped toward us. Giving it some gas, the Scout groaned and started to roll forward. It was clocking about thirty when I fell out.

The ground jumped up and smacked my face. I could taste dirt as I did a painful somersault.

The noble Scout swerved right as it bounced down the steep hill. It made it about a hundred feet before it hit a rock and started an end over end tumble. I didn't wait to watch it come to rest. It didn't look like I would be getting my deposit back from Jason B. But what the fuck, it didn't seem likely I'd be alive long enough for him to collect the forty grand from me.

"Give me ten, then get them out of here." My heart was doing triple time. The coke had joined the Viagra in its battle against the effects of the booze.

"He can't drive." Peter looked to Mikayla for support.

She shrugged.

The keys had been under the sun visors of both the panel van and the black Mercedes. After loading the girls into the van, I dropped into the German luxury cruiser. "I'll meet you at the plaza in Tecate." My voice sounded distant and much clearer than it felt.

"I don't think we will be seeing you," Mikayla said.

I wanted to puke. I wanted to fight the world. I turned the key.

CHAPTER 15

My jaw was pumping like a demon as I came down off the mountain. The Mercedes took the curves like a champ. I was on the flats when I saw headlights coming at me. I kept the speed down in deference to the Mercedes' less than manly suspension. The truck barreling at me had no such concerns. The gap between us was closing fast. A dry river bed lay between us, if I could make it down to sand, I'd have more room to maneuver without having to worry about another cactus killing my ride. I cranked the German V8 up, amazed at the instant access to torque. We were ten feet apart when I hit the riverbed. It was clear the madman powering at me had no intention of swerving. His high beams blinded me. With nothing to spare, I spun the wheel left. Sliding into the sand, sparks flew from where the vehicles scraped sides. Sluicing back onto the dirt road, I bounded up the opposite bank. The SUV disappeared behind me. Partly, I hoped he would spin around and give chase. A smaller voice hoped he would just keep going. Let Mikayla deal with his crazy ass.

I slowed down to a safe if not sane thirty MPH. At that speed, it didn't take long for the headlights to catch up. He was still doing well over sixty when he rear-ended the Mercedes. I jolted violently forward, but to my surprise the heavy German steed stayed on track. Six feet of flame leapt from the driver's window. A large bullet blasted a baseball sized hole in the rear window, then whizzed past my face and out through an equally scary hole punched into the windshield.

Ahead I could see the highway; it was tantalizingly close. I swerved to the left as he fired again. Dodging the lead, I spun back on the hard dirt inches before I struck a fallen oak. Fuck the suspension; it was time to lose this prick. Pushing the gas pedal to the floor, I was pressed back into my seat. The car bucked and slid, but with careful aim and a bit of muscle I was able to keep it in a straight line. The SUV's lights fought to keep up with me. He was concentrating too hard on driving to throw any more shots my way.

I was doing ninety when I hit the highway. I know they say to look both ways before crossing a road, but I never was one to listen. A bus blared its horn as I flew past it. The Mercedes was glued to the pavement. Crossing the highway, I nailed a hard left and headed back towards Ensenada. The SUV had to lock up his brakes to keep from smashing like a bug on the side of the bus. By the time he got across the road, I had dialed it up to well past a hundred. I don't know what ungodly amount the S500 cost, but it was worth every penny. It soared down the highway like a racehorse that had to be held back. Even at high speed it felt like it had mountains of thrust left. Pushing it up over the hundred and forty mark, the SUV's headlights shrunk to pin points and then were gone like a bad memory.

I dumped the car in a strip club parking lot, I left the keys in the ignition. It would be gone, stripped or painted before whoever was hunting us found it. Slipping down a dark alley I leaned against a brick wall. My heart was pounding. My head throbbed. My shoulder felt like it was on fire. My cock was still rock hard. I felt like throwing up. I had to keep moving.

I did a quick accounting and found a hundred and forty-two dollars, a SIG .380 with five rounds in the mag and nothing else. My duffle, extra cash and guns had gone down with the Scout. I was eighty miles from the border in Tecate, some mad fucker was hunting me and it wouldn't be long before the local cops started looking for the killer of three thugs in an alley and three more out at the hacienda. Even in these Wild West days, that many bodies would surely put them high on their list of crimes to solve. I was caked in sweat, dust and blood. I needed a doctor, a bath, a drink and a long night's sleep but it didn't look like I was going to be getting any of them any time soon.

Adolpho was sitting on his stool in front of Anthony's when I stumbled up. "Chingalo! You look bad, compadre."

"You think?" I tried to smile, but failed miserably.

"Are they looking for you?"

"Oh, yeah."

"Then come, rápido!" He led me around the side of the club to a small parking lot. Laying back the front seat of his Toyota, he placed a rough woven blanket over me and promised to come back as soon as his shift was over at four. He was afraid to draw attention to himself by leaving early.

In the dark car I closed my eyes, I couldn't shake the fear in Nika's face when I mounted her. The feel of her downy hair against my cock. My hand brushed across my erection. The faint scent of her sex was on me. I hadn't been laid in months and it had taken its toll. I started to stroke myself, anything to escape the reality of my situation. My stomach started to tumble. I was jerking off to thoughts of a child. Opening the car door I puked onto the asphalt. I was trembling with the blanket up over my head when sleep finally took me.

In the soft predawn light, Teyo sat in the park down by the bay. The massive Mexican flag flying overhead slapped in the morning breeze. One of the other tip boys passed him the fat joint. He had spent the night this way. After the shootout with the Russians, he had run deeper into the barrio. He used the cash the foreigners had fronted him to buy a bag of bud, the good shit, not the rag he normally smoked. This was the kind of weed he usually reserved to impress a girl. But he needed to chill, hang with his friends and blot out the ugliness.

None of the boys heard Xlmen approach, he seemed to appear standing before them. "You are called Teyo?" He pointed one of his gnarled fingers at the boy. Teyo nodded nervously. "Leave us." Xlmen looked at the others, who were quick to comply. One of them gave Teyo a sorry expression, but what could they do?

"Do you know who I am?" Xlmen asked once they were alone in the plaza.

"Si, señor, you are Santiago's hunter."

"Are you frightened?"

"No," Teyo lied.

"Then you are an idiot. I have killed more men than you have met."

"Are you going to kill me?" Even in the cold, Teyo had started to sweat.

"Most likely, yes. You have been working for the Russians."

"Just the one time, I swear on my mother's grave, I was going to tell Señor Santiago."

"You're a liar, I don't blame you. Truth has lost all value in these troubled times. Did you take a woman to meet with them?"

"No, only the two gringos, I swear."

"I know, on your mother's grave. Who was a toothless whore, I'm sure. Describe the gringos."

"The short one had glasses, skinny, I think he liked the coca, and glasses, he had glasses," Teyo started to relax. This was a task he was up to and maybe there would be some cash in it if he could help Santiago find the gringos.

"The other?"

"Big, very tall, and strong. Red hair and beard, I'm sure he has done time before, you can tell. His eyes, they were flat and he carried a huge gun. See my head, this lump he gave me." He parted his dirty black hair, turning around to show where his head had hit the wall. Xlmen drove his hunting knife into the boy's back, passing between the ribs and into the heart. A small gasp was the only sound Teyo made before he died.

Dreams, if they have any logic, it is lost on me. I'm standing in the living room of a wealthy home. Kittens are running around the floor, many kittens, maybe hundreds, it's hard to tell, they keep running back and forth. Something is wrong with them, some birth defect. They will never grow up to be happy, life will only get worse and worse for them. It is my job to kill these kittens, it is the only humane thing to do. In my hand is a hatchet. I bring it down, severing the first little creature's head. She is a small tabby, she could have fit in my hand with room to spare and now she is lifeless. I know I should feel bad, but I'm doing what must be done. Sometimes life isn't a pretty field of flowers, sometimes we have to do ugly acts to hold back worse ugliness. I take three more small heads quickly and easily, none struggle or cry out. They seem resigned to their fate. The blade of the hatchet comes down on an orange little fluff ball's neck, but it doesn't sever the head. The kitten screeches in pain. I swing down again, bones crunch but the crippled kitten isn't dead. She tries to crawl away from me. I keep chopping. My stomach turns sour. The kitten shrieks in an almost human voice.

A happy six year old brown-skinned boy stared down at me. The dream faded away, leaving me unsettled. I was in bed in Adolpho's house. I vaguely remembered him driving me, he had washed me in a large tub, gently as any mother had ever washed their child. A sticky mud paste covered my shoulder where the dog had bit me. My mouth tasted like a gym sock. When the boy noticed I was awake, he smiled and started asking me a string of questions in Spanish.

"No habla Español," I told him.

"No? I know Spanish, English and some French. Don't you go to school?"

"I went, but I wasn't much good at it."

"I'm first in my class."

"Smart kid."

"I know. Popi says you have a good heart, but bad judgment."

"Your popi said that?"

"Si, was he right?"

"Yes, he was right."

"Jaquene!" A short sturdy woman leaned in the door, she spoke in harsh Spanish. The boy rolled his eyes at me and then walked out. The woman leaned down, inspecting my shoulder. She prodded the tender flesh and sniffed it.

"Will I live?" I asked her.

"No, but this wound will not be your death." Her accent was thick, her voice was soft with an edge of steel resting just below the surface.

"You are Adolpho's woman?"

"His wife. I am not the innocent mountain girl he thinks I am. I know bad men when I see them. You repay kindness with death. I have fixed you as good as any hospital, now I want you gone from my house."

Adolpho snapped something in Spanish. She looked at her husband, shaking her head sadly, then left us alone.

"She's right, you know," I told him.

"No, Lorda sees the world in black and white, si? You are a malo hombre with bueno corazón, si? Gray is the color of our lives."

"If you say so." I didn't want to argue the point, but I was pretty sure I was a bad man with a bad heart. The list of evidence was growing longer every day.

Over a bowl of spicy stew, Adolpho told me that both the police and Santiago, a local crime boss, were looking for me. Apparently my good amigo the tip boy had sold me out. I told Adolpho I had to get to Tecate.

"La policía are watching the highway. Better you go south, get lost in Baja."

"I can't, people are counting on me, people I don't want to let down."

"The niña?"

"Yes."

"Through the mountains, muy peligroso, but possible."

"Can you draw me a map?"

"Oh hermano, it is dirt roads, trails, no map. I will take you."

"I don't want to put you in danger."

"Then don't tell Lorda." His mind was made up, nothing I could say would change it.

Santiago sat drinking an espresso while Xlmen gave his report. The roads were sealed, the Mercedes found in town, but there had been no sign of the big gringo or the tarot card killer. "The puta is dead, but doesn't know it yet. They are here somewhere, I will find them."

"Certainly," Santiago said, "but how many of our people will die before that day comes? The Russians paid us a lot for protection, now they are dead. This is not good. Someone is hiding these people. Find out who and you will find them." Ensenada was in many ways a small town, Santiago knew if he pressed hard enough, someone would talk. And who was better at pressing than Xlmen?

On the outskirts of Ensenada, we stopped at a small, one pit garage. Adolpho's cousin climbed out from under a rusted Chevy truck. His coveralls were streaked with black grease stains, and when he shook my hand it felt rough and calloused from years behind a wrench.

"You not so big," he said looking me over.

"Excuse me?"

"I heard the gringo they were looking for was a giant."

"Must be someone else, I'm here on vacation."

"Ok, sure, whatever you say." His grin told me he wasn't buying it. Adolpho traded his Toyota to his cousin for an older 4x4 pickup. When asked where we were going, he said vaguely, "The hills."

Heading into the eastern mountains, the pot-holed pavement became rutted dirt. Buoyant banda music floated out of the truck's radio, Adolpho sang along as if he hadn't a care in the world. I rolled a poncho he had given me and rested my head against the window and tried to sleep. My head wouldn't shut up. I kept seeing ugly images of dead Russians and a naked young girl. The fear in her eyes, the pain as I entered her. I needed a drink, I needed oblivion.

"What will you do with the niñas once you get to the

States?" Adolpho asked.

"Take them to LA, figure it out from there."

"Better not to worry about the end, at the beginning of the journey?"

"Something like that." In a life where tomorrow wasn't even close to guaranteed, it seemed wise not to get too far ahead of myself. I didn't have any idea how we were going to get them across, let alone what we would do with them then. But if I wound up in a Mexican jail behind a murder rap, any time spent planning for the girls would be wasted.

The sun was setting when we dropped down out of the mountains and found our way onto pavement again. One of the more striking aspects of Tecate was its lack of gringos. It was a border town without the corruption and sin that Americans bring or come for. Parking by the large open plaza, Adolpho started to get out. I told him he had to go home, my future was fucked, his didn't have to be. I thanked him for all he had done and took his address and promised to write. As I stepped away, he clasped my hand, pressing a small wad of pesos on me.

"Take it, no mucho, but maybe it helps." Before I could refuse, he drove away. Why had he risked so much for a stranger? Did he have a daughter or sister who had been taken? Maybe he was one of those good men who do right, simply because it's right. In the joint we called guys like him chumps, soft touches without the brains it took to see the angles.

Before going to look for the others, I went to a barbershop. A jolly Spanish-speaking gent gave me a shave and a haircut for slightly more than two bits. Twelve bucks more bought me a white straw cowboy hat and a pair of Ray-Ban knock offs. Adolpho's poncho completed the transformation. I didn't look like a Mexican, but I also didn't look like an LA hood. If my description was on the wire, I hoped this would be enough to keep me from being nabbed.

A band was playing bouncy Spanish music in the center of the plaza. From benches, husbands and wives watched their kids running on the grass. Vendors lined up to sell leather goods, trinkets and food. Teenagers clustered under spreading tree branches to smoke and laugh. The whole scene had the feeling of Main Street USA in the fifties, as if the American small town dream hadn't been lost, it just moved south.

I walked past a young man in a denim work coat, his CAT trucker's hat pulled down over his eyes. It wasn't until she called my name that I recognized it was Mikayla.

I sat on the bench a few feet from her and spoke without looking in her direction, "Did everyone make it?"

"Yes, the girls are in a motel, not far." Her eyes scanned the plaza for any sign of trouble.

"Peter?" I asked.

"Left to make arrangements for transportation. Were you followed?"

"I doubt it. We really pissed off some Mexican crime boss, Santiago?"

"Good, the man is a pimp, deserves a slow death." She rose and walked away. I let her get a hundred yard lead then set out after her. If either of us had a shadow, this was our best chance of discovering it. She took us on a circuitous walking tour of Tecate, only after she was good and sure we had no tail did she go to the Motel Rosa. It was an old fashioned motor court; low single story buildings ringing a parking lot. The girls were in room 13, the number might have bothered me if I thought my luck could get any worse. As it stood, any luck would be good luck.

The girls were dressed in matching blue running suits, their makeup had been scrubbed off and their hair was tied back. They looked more like a high school track team than the baby hookers we had rescued the night before. Mikayla told me it had been Peter's idea, he had crossed the border and bought the outfits at a Target. I was starting to like this guy, or at least recognize he wasn't totally useless. The girls were focused on the TV, watching me from the corners of their eyes. At their feet lay the remnants of a McDonald's feast, another of Peter's gifts I was sure.

Nika rested in one of the two double beds. Her foot had been bandaged. Her color had gone from gray to a more natural shade of pale. I was ashamed to look at her. She looked up at me, wanting to say something, but what could be said? The uncomfortable silence was broken by the sound of a key turning in the lock. Peter stepped in, he was in a blue tracksuit that matched the girls', it had COACH stitched over his heart, a silver whistle hung around his neck.

"You are full of surprises," I grinned, looking over his disguise.

"McGuire. Figured you for road kill when I saw that truck take out after you."

"Almost was, would it have been better for the story if I had died?"

"Yes, more dramatic, a real tearjerker. 'Brave American vigilante going down in flames to protect beautiful Russian girls.' Brief bio on you, leaving out the jail time, of course. Yeah, it smells of Peabody."

"I could go back and let him kill me if you want."

"No, by now it would just be gratuitous. Besides, I've got a feeling you may have a few more story twists in you."

"We'll see. So Coach, what's the plan?"

It was simple and clean, Peter had rented a GMC Yukon, as vanilla a ride as any on the road. He was going to drive across the border like any other American returning from a day trip to good old Mexico. Homeland Security and the President's "Arm the Border" plan mandated passport checks, but the feds hadn't funded any extra help, so here in the frontier, the border patrol only looked for illegals of the brown skin type or drug smugglers. Coach and his girls didn't fit either profile.

Mikayla and I on the other hand, vibed trouble and all the costumes in the world wouldn't change that.

Peter agreed to take the girls across, if they got caught, his position with the press could help keep them out of jail. Maybe even get them refugee status. If he made it, he would take them to Helen's Silver Lake home and wait for us.

As they drove away, Nika looked out the back window. She reminded me of Anya; I had seen those same scared, resigned eyes looking at me out the back of a Mercedes before. What crime had these sisters ever done to bring the world down on them? The only one I could see was their desire for a better life, that and the crime of being born beautiful.

From across the street, Mikayla and I watched the Yukon move with a line of cars toward the border. Hawkers moved between the cars offering one last chance to buy crap trinkets. Three cars in front of them, a mobile home was motioned by the man in a khaki uniform to pull into the search lane. Two more border guards moved around the huge camper, looking under it with mirrors. Two clean cut grandparents stepped down, the man was saying something that didn't look like pleasantries. Apparently, he was not real happy at being chosen for the search.

Two cars were waved through and then it was Peter's turn. He rolled down the window at the gate. Leaning out, he said something. He was smiling like an idiot. The officer looked in the back at the girls, then at Peter. I held my breath. The officer waved Peter though. The Yukon's brake lights went out and they drove into America.

"Now comes the hard part," I said, looking at Mikayla.

"Not so hard, you have papers?"

"The federales are looking for us."

"And you decided not to tell me until now?"

"Thought if Peter knew, he might not go." I told her about the tip boy and the Ensenada police. We agreed walking across legally was out of the question. If the Mexicans didn't grab us, the US customs would. We were wanted for a string of murders, and even though they all deserved to die, I didn't really want to try and explain that to a Mexican judge.

CHAPTER 16

In the plaza we bought dinner from a pushcart, tamales, fresh steamed corn sprinkled with chili powder, and a couple Fanta's. "You've got clean papers, no one knows what you look like," I told Mikayla. "I think it's best if you cross over and I'll meet you in LA."

"What makes you think I'm going to LA?" She was picking corn from her teeth with her pinky nail.

"It's going to be hot for you down here, I figured you might want to head north."

"It's hot wherever I go."

"Yeah, you do seem to leave a bloody trail."

"I am going to LA. Those things we killed in Ensenada, their boss is in LA. I'm tired of hacking at the snake's tail."

"I'll give you Gregor's address, he'll give you what we know."

"You will take me to him yourself." She finished her orange soda in two long gulps.

"I don't know how I'm getting across."

"I know, but it should be fun watching you try."

"You know I'm a man, right?"

"Yes, and the first I haven't wanted to kill in a long time, so don't press your luck. Now finish eating, we have a long night ahead of us." If she knew what I had done to Nika, she would have slit my throat and left my body to rot.

The blat of unbaffled mufflers sounded as we crossed the plaza. Four dust covered teenage gringos rounded the corner on dirt bikes. I picked up the pace, following their sound after they turned down a side street. A block from the plaza we found them, parked in front of The Drunken Coyote. It was a tourist bar that, judging from the parking lot, catered to the off-road crowd.

Keeping to the shadows, we moved through the parking lot. "If you see anyone coming, whistle," I told Mikayla, as I slipped into a topless jeep.

"What are you looking for?"

"A map." She nodded, needing no more explanation. It took three more tries before I found what I was looking for, in the pouch behind the driver's seat of a Baja bug was a topographic map with dirt trails highlighted in yellow. I stole the map, a small flashlight and a compass that had been glued to the dash.

It was just past nine, with any luck the boys on the dirt bikes would be drinking until two or three. By then we could be deeply lost in the Tecate Mountains. The fork locks broke with one mighty twist of the handlebars. We wheeled the bikes out the back of the parking lot and down a quiet street; a Mexican man watched us roll past his front porch, he said nothing.

Borrowing a blade from my favorite assassin, I stripped two wires and in less than ten seconds, the engines were rattling to life. When I asked Mikayla if she knew how to ride, she sneered at me, apparently motorcycles were the main mode of transport in the Ukraine.

At a Pemex station we filled the tanks, Mikayla bought a pack of smokes and after studying the map, we chose what looked like the best route. Thirty-six hard miles and we would be in San Diego.

"Bandits patrol the wasteland," Mikayla said flatly. "And Mexican soldiers, DEA choppers, the Border Patrol."

"Anyone else?"

"American vigilantes, angry ranchers."

"That it?"

"Yes, I think that's it."

"Piece of chocolate cake." I shot her a grin and pulled out onto the road. The bike felt good between my legs, I hadn't ridden since selling my Norton, I forgot how free and safe I felt on two wheels. Five miles west of town, we found the first dirt road. We bounced our way up a steep path, dodging the small pines and rock outcroppings.

Holding the front wheel straight on the bumping trail brought fresh pain to my shoulder. I could feel the dried poultice cracking under the movement. Stopping to check the map, I let my arm hang down, hoping to relax the bruised muscles.

We missed the cutoff on the first pass and had to back

track half a mile. It was a thin walking trail, swinging down into a small dry valley and then up into the mountains again. We killed the bikes, looking down. This was the frontier, once past the mountains, on the other side we would be on US soil, not that it meant much No one painted a dotted line on the ground, in the wilderness the border was much mushier than in the city where they used ten-foot chain link and razor wire as demarcation. Out here, Mexico and the US bled into one another for a couple of miles in either direction, not legally, but in reality. The rule of the gun reigned. Attorneys, courts and politicians began their rule once past the jagged mountains.

In the west, we spotted a chopper flying low, spotlighting the ground below it. If they were going to nail us, it would be in the valley. Taking off my shirt, I wrapped it around the headlight. Out of her rucksack, Mikayla took a tee shirt and followed my lead. We waited, watching the chopper, scanning the dark mountains for any movement. Without the sun, the air temperature plummeted. I wrapped Adolpho's poncho around myself and rubbed the muscles around the dog bite.

Mikayla lit a butt, cupping it in her hand to hide the cherry. Hunched down she looked at peace, eyes alert but not nervous. She was comfortable waiting. I used to be like that, now whenever I stopped moving, my head filled with voices. Voices of the dead or walking wounded. Whisky had always shut the damn voices up. Now court was in session 24/7 and only forward movement would hush their harsh judgment.

The chopper rose and floated off towards the dim city lights in the west.

"Let's ride," I said.

"No, wait." She lit a second coffin nail. After a bit, we saw it - down in the valley, a small group of shadows distinguished themselves from a grove of cypress. They moved across the floor of the valley. We waited another minute until we were sure that our fellow travelers hadn't brought the Border Patrol swooping down out of the hills.

Kicking over the small engines, they sounded like machine gun fire against the night's silence. The trail switched back and forth across the steep incline. A half hour later, we finally reached flat ground. The trail rambled through the chaparral, dodging scrub oaks, cypress and boulders. Our covered headlights lit enough of the path to keep us from collision if we kept the speed down.

Without warning, Mikayla powered up beside me, twisting her handlebar to the left, she forced me off the path. Brush tore at my legs as I bounced down a shallow gully. She was close beside me when I pulled the bike to a stop. I was about to yell at her when she leaned in and shut my motor off. Jumping off her bike, she caught me mid shoulders. I tumbled back, landing on the hard dry earth. Her hand was over my mouth and she was on top of me. I had enough time to wonder if a razor was coming next before I heard the roar of an engine.

Headlights bounced on the branches above us. Through the brush I could see a pickup speeding down the path. A light bar on the roof illuminated a wide circle around them. Over the cab, between the lights, two men stood. I could clearly see the outline of a rifle held by one of them.

Reaching in my pocket, I took hold of the pistol. My muscles tensed, readying to leap up. Mikayla's breath was warm and shallow on my face, I could feel her heart beating against my chest. Her pale blue eyes glowed with intensity. How had I ever mistaken her for a boy? The scar running from ear to lip stood in defiance of her fine features. Strong cheek bones, an elegant nose and thin but perfectly shaped lips. Women, even with the possibility of death rolling toward me, I still marveled at the draw they had on my attention.

The pickup passed close enough for me to read the tread on monster mud tires. The man with the rifle had a bandanna over his nose and mouth, a defense against the dust storm they were stirring up. Glare reflected from the light bar on his goggles, making him appear inhuman.

"Bandits," Mikayla said when they had passed, "people crossing bring every cent they have, to start their new lives. These vultures pick them clean." Noticing her hand was still covering my mouth, she removed it. She seemed uncomfortable with our closeness. Climbing quickly off my chest, she turned her back to me. Staying low, she watched the receding taillights.

The report of a rifle echoed against the mountain walls. Mikayla was up, kicking over her bike before the last reverberation died away. Ripping the cover off the headlight she was bounding up onto the trail while I stumbled to get my bike started.

Half way across the valley, the truck stood, a glowing beacon. Mikayla sped towards them. Cranking back the throttle, I felt the front tire fighting to come up off the ground. Pushing up from the pegs, I leaned forward, keeping my weight over the front fork. Swerving around the spikes of saguaros, I skidded my foot on the ground for balance. Banging my boot off the rocks I was glad my Docs had steel toes. The path rose enough to see that in the light surrounding the truck, a group of tattered Mexicans were on their knees, four armed men stood over them. I had time to register a woman clutching what looked like a child to her chest before I dipped down and they disappeared from view.

I was a hundred feet behind Mikayla when she reached

the truck. The men turned, shock caught on their faces as her headlight struck them. They were swinging guns up when she blurred through them with one of her arms stretched out from her body. Something glinted in her hand, then she was past them. The man in the bandanna fell to his knees, clutching his neck, fighting to staunch the blood cascading down his chest. The other three spun and opened fire at her. Muzzle flashes lit the scene, flickering like some demonic strobe light.

Twisting the throttle fully open, I aimed at the back of the biggest of the men. Pulling the front wheel into the air, I watched in slow motion, his body came closer, shells popped from his M16.

The people on the ground huddled down seeking safety in the dirt.

The crunch of bone sounded when my tire collided with his flesh. He fell forward. The handlebars ripped from my hands. The bike flipped away from me. I hit the ground rolling. Bullets pocked the earth around me as I tumbled.

Mikayla's headlights flashed back on the remaining men. Drawing their fire, she raced toward them. They arced their barrels at her.

I slid to a stop. Digging in my pocket, I found the pistol.

Bullets sparked off Mikayla's bike. She tumbled back, hitting the ground.

Holding the small pistol in both hands to steady my aim, I pulled the trigger. It sounded like a firecracker, with almost no recoil. Two slugs ripped into one man's face. I turned on the other and dumped three shots into his chest before the automatic's breach locked open.

I could hear a bike's engine and its tire spinning uselessly in the air, a man's moan, a woman's prayers muttered in Spanish.

Running to the fallen bandits, I kicked a rifle away from the only one still breathing. He was hugging himself, letting out short guttural gasps. A woman holding a baby wrapped in a serape watched me without moving. I ran out into the chaparral, toward where Mikayla had fallen.

She was laying in a sandy patch of ground on her back. As I neared, I saw the shallow movement of her chest. Kneeling over her, she looked up at me. She was breathing slowly through her nostrils. Pulling open her jacket, I looked for signs of blood, but found none.

"Are they dead?" she whispered.

"All but one and I doubt he'll last long."

"Good."

I sat in the sand and watched her as her breaths grew in depth. It wasn't long before she could sit up. I was glad to see she hadn't broken her back or any other bones. It would hurt like hell in the morning but she would live, if I didn't come to my senses and kill her first. "Next time," I said quietly, "you mind asking me before committing my ass to a suicide run?"

"They needed us." Her voice was coming back.

"I have people back in LA, my people, who count on me making it back alive."

"They're all my people." Her blue eyes flashed ice.

"You a saint? Or a lunatic? Some kind of Mother Teresa with a razor?"

"No, I am whatever I am, this is what I do. If you can't handle it, we split up now."

"And miss the fun of seeing what you do next? Fuck, no."

The last of the bandits had choked on his own blood while I was with Mikayla. The travelers were still huddled on the ground; they watched us with frightened eyes. How could they know if we had come to help or rob or kill them? In this unforgiving wasteland, good Samaritans were few and far between.

Mikayla picked over the corpses while I searched the truck. I found a bottle of tequila, a rat-eared porn magazine and not much more. Mikayla had better luck, their pockets had produced a small wad of pesos and their hands had given up two gold rings and a watch.

After depositing her booty into her rucksack, Mikayla spoke to the travelers. Rising, they solemnly shook her hand and moved to the truck. Piling in, they started out across the valley, heading toward America. None had even looked at me, I think they were afraid I might go crazy and kill them. They had mistaken my size for danger and Mikayla's gender for kindness. Or maybe they had seen the truth in us.

Cleaning my prints off the pistol, I tossed it out into the dark landscape. The bandits hadn't offered up any arms smaller than a rifle, and I didn't think the highway patrol would look too kindly on my strapping one of them on my back. I hated the idea of traveling without firepower, but I had no choice. Mikayla was placing her tarot cards on the bodies when I discovered that bullets had punctured her bike's gas tank and shattered the carburetor. "Maybe we should have taken the truck," I said.

"They needed it more than us."

"Whatever you say, Mother Mikayla." Against her will, she smiled slightly at my nickname. She arched an eyebrow at me when I slipped the tequila into her rucksack, but she didn't say anything.

Climbing on behind me, she wrapped her arms around my waist. I didn't bother cloaking the light, speed was what was needed now. I wanted to put as many miles between us and the dead men as quickly as possible. I wasn't really worried about the cops, these hills were scattered with the bones of dead travelers. Reporting a body meant paperwork and one more unsolved case on the books. Most of the fallen lay where they died. Coyotes and vultures would feed off the carrion and the circle of life would continue to spin.

Mikayla was the perfect passenger, she crushed her body into my back, bending when I did, shifting her weight along with mine. The warmth of her breath moved across the back of my neck where her face was pressed. It was nice to feel her there, not that I had much time to think on it, all my concentration was used to keep us on the track while I blasted us across the valley floor.

A half mile up the mountain, we passed the pickup. In the back, the young mother watched me. Her flat Indian face was solid and strong, her eyes held neither gratitude nor fear for me. I was simply one more event in her short, long life. Something in her strength and way she held the child to her made me glad she was coming to my home country. We needed more like her, people with the will to survive the hard strange days our country seemed destined for. Greed and dishonor were tearing at the bones of America and if we had any hope, it would come from women like this solid mother who would risk so much for so little. In my head, I could hear Bono singing about climbing mountains and searching for that unfound dream. I hoped these travelers would find what they were looking for.

An hour later, we were down in the far southern corner of Anza-Borrego National Park land. We had made it to US soil and although the Border Patrol worked the area, two Anglos on a dirt bike wouldn't raise their suspicions, even looking like we did. The desert was used to freaks, hell it collected them. The temperature had dropped below freezing when I rolled to a stop and leaned against a Joshua tree's rough bark.

"Give me that tequila," I said to Mikayla.

"You sure this is the time? We aren't home yet."

"We're never home, you and me." I twisted the cap off, the smell screamed drink me. Peeling my shirt off my shoulder, it took a good hunk of scab and flesh with it. I clenched my jaw to keep from yelling. Pouring the tequila onto the wound set it on fire.

"Here." Mikayla handed me a clean pair of cotton underpants, granny panties as the strippers called them. "If you don't scrub it, it will fester." She didn't offer to help me. If I had asked her to, I'm sure she would have, but to offer would have said she didn't think I could handle my own problems. It was a sign of respect, not a dismissal of my pain.

I don't know which was worse, cleaning the wound or not drinking the tequila. Mikayla handed me her last clean shirt to tear into a makeshift bandage. Laying down with her rucksack as a pillow, she smoked, looking up into the sky. It was late, the thought of any more jostling miles that night seemed impossible. We agreed to sleep until sun up and then head for

Joshua Tree, take the desert and avoid the San Diego border patrol check points.

Sitting against the tree trunk, I looked up at the star glutted sky. It was a carpet of pinpoints, those stars felt so close I thought I could reach out and touch them. The cold was biting, but at least I wasn't on that damn bike.

"Come here," Mikayla's voice was soft, almost gentle. "Lay down beside me, body warmth will keep us from freezing." I knew she was letting me closer than any man in many years. I was honored and also thankful for the warmth as she pulled close to me. I draped the poncho over us and we shared her rucksack pillow. Tilting my face so that we were nose to nose I ran my finger over her scar. I don't know where I got the courage to touch her in such a personal way. Maybe it was exhaustion, or maybe it was the softening in her eyes. I felt her body tense when I touched her, but she didn't pull away.

"Who did this to you?" I whispered.

"I did." Her voice was so soft that even in the silent desert night I had to strain to hear her. "In one summer, fourteen girls were taken from my village, taken to be sold as prostitutes. The men came with guns and KGB badges. Anyone who stood in their way was killed. They took my only sister, my father tried to stop them. He died that night. They only wanted pretty girls, so I made myself ugly." Lifting her shirt, she showed me her bare chest. She closed her eyes, unable to watch me seeing her shame. A long jagged scar ran from her collarbone down to where her left breast had been. The scar spider webbed where her nipple should have been. "I nearly bled to death before the doctor could repair what I had done." She shivered from more than cold as I traced the scar tissue. Her right breast was small and perfect, I wanted to kiss it, lick her pink erect nipple. I pulled her shirt down and pulled her closer.

Rolling onto her side, she spooned into me, pulling my arm around her. We drifted off to sleep like that. It was the first time in many moons that I wasn't wracked by my bad dreams. Somehow she made me feel both safe and protective at the same time. With my arms around this strange damaged killer, I felt as if I wasn't a bad man or a good man, I just was.

In the gray predawn, I awoke. Mikayla was sleeping in my arms. The desert stretched out around us, empty and peaceful. The pain in my shoulder had subsided into a dull ache. When I moved my arm, Mikayla snapped into consciousness. She popped her elbow back, catching me in the bridge of my nose. Rolling away, she leapt up ready to fight me.

"Whoa, Killer, it's me, Moses. Remember?" I felt the warm trickle of blood flowing from my nostrils.

"Oh, no." She looked at what she had done.

"Forget it."

"I thought..." She let it hang in the air, unfinished.

"Been broken before, but never by so pretty a lady." She looked away, stung by the compliment. The softness that had overtaken her at night was gone, her shields were up now. She looked out across the barren desertscape, her back to me.

Standing, I stretched to loosen the kinks the hard ground had given me. Wiping my face on my shirtsleeve, I removed the blood.

"Let's ride." I kicked over the bike. Mikayla climbed on behind me, pulling herself close.

"I'm sorry," she whispered into my ear as I took off.

We dumped the bike outside of Twentynine Palms. It wasn't street-legal, and it was hot. Not a good combination if we wanted a casual entrance into LA. We bought two tickets on the next bus to Los Angeles, and spent the next hour in a small diner eating steaks and eggs, and sharing a pot of coffee. We didn't talk about the night before, her scars, the tenderness I felt for her. We ate instead in silence.

From a pay phone, I called Helen. Peter had arrived safely, he had then locked himself in Helen's den and been on her computer ever since. There had been no time on the road for notes, he was reconstructing the events and attempting to write the story while it was still fresh.

Helen told me the girls were fine, a bit freaked out, but other than that, fine. She had been working the phones, calling on contacts to find out what to do with them. "There's a group called Project Angel, out of Moscow, they have a local chapter. They work with trafficked girls. They may have some ideas," she said.

"Sounds good. Tell Peter I'll be around tonight, and Helen, watch your back. These Russian bastards aren't going to be overjoyed with any of us for what we did down in Mexico." After I hung up with her, I tried Gregor's cell but got voice mail. His mother's phone rang without being picked up. I knew Gregor could handle himself, but it still worried me. He should have picked up his phone.

Mikayla sank down into the soft seat on the bus. For the next few hours we were safe, there was nothing to do but try to relax and not worry about what was coming. Putting her hand on mine, she looked out the window. "I've never been with a man," she said to the glass.

"Don't think you've missed much."

"I like you, Moses, but I don't..."

"You don't have to do anything. I'm too old to date, and too tired to fuck." Leaning my head back, I let my eyes drift closed.

CHAPTER 17

Downtown LA is a human cesspool. By day, it's populated by high roller power boys of the stock market, lawyers and political creeps. At night, the art-damaged hipsters and twenty-something slum Sinatras take over. And around them all swirl the homeless, the sad, broken, forgotten men and women. Some came here by choice, others were driven by madness or addiction. This was where you ended up when you ran out of gas, looks or luck.

In the bus station, I tried Gregor again without any luck. I called Piper at home, got her machine and dialed Club Xtasy. When Doc answered, he wanted to know where the fuck I was and when I was coming back to work. Turaj was still in the hospital, Gregor was MIA and Doc was pulling doubles. "I'm not sure Uncle Manny wants me back. Now put Piper on the line."

"She's on stage, you want her to call you?" He sounded petulant, which isn't pretty on a large bald black man.

"I don't care if she's blowing the Pope's ghost. Get her on the phone." I could hear him shouting for her. It was still early, I doubted if they had more than two customers.

"This better be important." Piper was out of breath. From her tone of voice, I would have bet one hip was cocked and her fist was on it.

"It's me, baby."

"Mo, where the hell are you?"

"Have you heard from Gregor?"

"No, he's not answering his cell, I don't hear dick from him, from you. What the fuck's going on?"

"I'm at the bus station, downtown. I need a ride. Come get me and I'll tell you everything."

"What, you never heard of a cab?"

"I'm broke." It wasn't exactly true. Between Mikayla and me, we had a small fortune in pesos. And under twenty bucks in greenbacks. It took some more sweet tough talk, but Piper finally agreed. Doc would give her a ration of crap for leaving, but she could handle him. One of her killer smiles and the big guy would be a puddle on the floor. Mikayla was watching me when I hung up.

"Do you have many girlfriends?"

"Some, not like that, though."

"Why not like that?"

"They won't have me."

"I don't think that's true." She was looking at me as if I was some sort of interesting alien creature.

I walked up the block, hoping to find a currency exchange. Found several guys wanting to sell me chiva and a Korean man selling short dogs from a rusted shopping cart. But no one was willing to trade pesos for dollars.

Mikayla stood on the corner smoking. The sea of human sadness washed around her. She watched them without judgment. She'd seen worse places.

Fifteen minutes after the phone call, a white panel van threaded its way through the traffic towards us. Two dark skinned men sat in the front, the passenger was scanning the sidewalk with a little too much concentration for my comfort.

I stepped to the curb, when the man in van saw me he froze for the briefest moment, but it was long enough for me to know it was me he was looking for.

"This is wrong, let's go," I told Mikayla as I rushed past her. I heard tires squealing as we rounded the corner. Over my shoulder, the white van skidded through traffic. At the next corner, I turned up a one way street. It was going the opposite direction.

The van slid to a stop and four men jumped out of the side door. They were dressed in jeans and windbreakers and looked Middle Eastern.

We had a block lead when we hit Broadway. The crush of quitting traffic slowed the streets to a crawl and flooded the sidewalks. I plowed through the pedestrians with Mikayla running in my wake. A red Metro sign glowed ahead of us. Swinging down the stairs, I pushed my way down into the subway. We hit the red line just as the train pulled in. We were swept into the car with the swarm of commuters. As the train pulled away, I saw the dark skinned men moving on the platform, searching the crowd for us.

When we hit the dark of the tunnel, I looked at the map to see where we were headed. Hollywood, that would do fine. Any place with crowds to get lost in.

"What did we do to piss off the Arabs?" I asked Mikayla as we stood rumbling along.

"Israeli, I think they were Israeli," she said.

"If you say so. Why are they after us?"

"I don't know." She was hiding something.

"Have anything to do with that whorehouse fire in Tel Aviv Peter was talking about?"

"Maybe." She didn't elaborate.

"Any other baggage you want to tell me about? Mexicans, Russians, Israelis... anyone else want to kill you? What about the Canadians, you ever do anything to them?" People in the car were starting to stare. I didn't care.

"You know who I am. You know what I do," she said softly.

By the time we reached the Highland station, my adrenaline had eased up enough for me to think a bit more clearly. Moving through the happy tourists in front of Grauman's Chinese Theater felt completely surreal. A towhead boy put his feet over Bogart's cement footprints while his mother snapped a picture. I winced with every flash bulb, reminded of the guns in the borderland. Mikayla took it all in with her same stoic calmness.

I found a cab in front of the Roosevelt Hotel, gave the

driver an address in North Hollywood. I spent the entire ride watching for white vans and black Mercedes, LA had never looked less like home.

"Where the fuck is my truck?" Jason B was not a happy camper to see me walk up without the Scout. The cabby had been convinced to take the last of our US dollars and a small stack of pesos, he let us off up the block from Jason B's shop. I had left Mikayla on the street, no need for Jason B to see her with me.

"Gone."

"Gone? Gone? Forty grand's worth of rolling stock, and all you can say is 'gone'?"

"I need the Crown Vic."

"How the fuck are you planning to pay for this destruction? You got cash? Didn't think so. Fuck!"

"You know I'm good for it." I was trying to remain calm.

"No, what I know is you look like a fucking bum on his last bad run. What I know is I'm out a primo ride worth a wedge of cash and now you want another car. Do I look like your bitch? You see a dress on me?" Spittle flew from his lips.

"Go get my keys before I forget I like you." I kept my eyes flat and my voice even.

"You threatening me?" He was trying to keep his bravado up, but I could see a crack of fear appearing under it.

"It's been a rough couple days, one more body won't dent my karma one way or the other, so get my keys."

"Alright, big man, chill, I know you're good for it." He

reached into his desk drawer. I grabbed the drawer, pinning his hand inside it. He let out a small yelp. With one hand locked on his wrist, I opened the drawer; in his hand was a Beretta 9mm. He looked up at me with a sheepish grin. I backhanded him hard enough to knock him off his chair.

"Deal remains the same," I said, towering over him. "I take my car, I will make good on the Scout."

He was finished, tail between his legs. He found the keys and led me to the Crown Vic. "I tuned her up, and she has a full tank." His eyes wouldn't meet mine.

"I'll see you around, Jason." Climbing behind the wheel, it felt good to be back in the road beast.

On the street, I picked up Mikayla and drove to a liquor store to make a call. Gregor was still not answering his cell and there was no answer at his mother's. We drove to Glendale without speaking. I slipped Dropkick Murphys into the stereo, Celtic punk to take my mind off worrying. *Cruel* came on; no, they weren't the Pogues, but they would do. I was glad to see Jason had left my CDs unharmed, if he hadn't, I might have had to waste his skinny ass.

If they had gotten to Gregor, they would have his house under surveillance. I parked two streets away from the pre-war court and we worked our way across backyards. Mikayla must have felt my tension, the razor was in her hand. The front door to Gregor's mother's cottage was splintered at the jamb. Gripping the Beretta, I pushed the door open. The living room was a mess, the coffee table had been upended, a china hutch lay on its side, spilling out a broken teacup collection. The bedroom was empty and untouched. There were more signs of struggle in the kitchen, plates with half-eaten breakfast were scattered on the floor. Under the table was a smear of blood, bullet holes pocked the floor.

"No, no, no, no." I stared at the blood stain.

Mikayla picked up a spent 9mm shell, reading the imprint on the bottom, "IMI, Israeli military."

"Israelis? FUCK. I don't give a fuck if they're Martians. They're dead men." A smeared trail of blood ran out the back door. We followed the scuffed brown tracks across the small yard and into the garage.

Folded up behind a dented Toyota, I found them. An elderly woman curled up, holding a bloody Bullmastiff. She covered her face. Guarding from the blow she was sure was coming.

Dropping to my knees, I clutched Angel, burying my face in her blood stiff fur. She was warm and I could feel her chest pulling shallow breaths. Her eyes rolled open, looked up at me, begging me for relief.

Mikayla helped Gregor's mother gently to her feet. All the blood on her was Angel's. While I held the dog, feeling for her wounds, I heard them speaking. When Gregor had seen the strangers coming, he had sent his mother out the back and told her to hide. That nice Russian girl had been in the shower. The old woman had heard gunshots and screaming. She obeyed her son and stayed hidden. Late in the night, she had crept into the house and found the dog. Gregor would come for them. He always did. She had been hiding all night and all day. She knew he would come for her.

"Who the heck has been using a beautiful bitch like this for target practice?" Bernie was a cross-dressing vet I had met in

Lebanon. I had saved his ass, literally. He owed me. He was a good man for a freak. He'd keep his mouth shut.

"Don't let her die."

"She's not looking real good."

"Just don't let her die."

We took Gregor's mom to a sister's house in the Valley and promised to have Gregor call her. She didn't ask me to save her son, she assumed he wouldn't need it. She believed in him that deeply.

Driving back down the 5, I tried to quiet the rage and think.

"Can you turn that noise off?" Mikayla asked, lighting a butt.

"No. It relaxes me." The Clash's *Give 'em Enough Rope* was rattling the windows. It gave my anger someplace to go while I tried to think. Who had taken Gregor and Anya? The same bastards shot my dog. They had to die. No, ease off. Think. The white haired Russian. Who else? Israelis. Minutes after I spoke to Piper, the white van came hunting me. PIPER. Fuck. Piper.

"This stripper, is she your girlfriend?" Mikayla asked as we waited down the street from Club Xtasy.

"Did I fuck her? Is that what you want to know?"

"I don't care who you have or have not fucked. What I want to know is will you be ok questioning her, or should I do it?"

"Questioning?"

"You know what that means." She was right, I did. I thought about her question without answering. Mikayla had made it clear the only thing she hated worse than pimps were those she called collaborators, women who sold out their gender for personal gain. She had a simple worldview that only included three types of people, victims, bad men and collaborators. I knew it was much more complicated than that. Most of the world was populated by noncombatants, men and women who were just trying to make it from birth to grave with the least amount of pain.

At 2:15 the girls came out, with Doc standing guard from the top of the stairs. He watched until they were safely to their cars. Piper got into her baby blue Ford Falcon. When she pulled out I counted to twenty and then rolled out after her. I gave her a long leash, figuring she would be heading home. I wanted to brace her in a non-public place, limit the chance of the cops getting involved.

Ten minutes later, she was unlocking the door to her small Silver Lake house. I hit the door and pushed in before she could lock it.

"Moses, what the hell?" She gasped as Mikayla closed and dead-bolted the door.

"Who the fuck are you working for?" I was screaming. She reached in her purse. I slapped it out of her hand. A small canister of mace rolled out onto the floor.

"What happened downtown, Piper?"

"You tell me. I left a suit worth two hundred bucks in lap dances, drove down there, waited in that creepy neighborhood and you never showed. Who is she?"

"Don't fucking lie to me, girl." I wanted to grab her throat. Gripping her kitchen table, I tossed it across the small room. "I'm running crazy, real unpredictable. If I don't get the truth this whole deal gets ugly fast. Who did you tell?"

Looking into my eyes, I could see fear taking hold of her. "What happened Mo? It's me, talk to me."

"Who did you tell?" I kept the intensity up, moving into her face.

"No one, Mo, believe me, no one."

"Bullshit. Somebody knew and you're the only one I spoke to."

"I didn't tell anyone, only Uncle Manny, he wanted to know why I was leaving in the middle of my shift."

"Manny?"

"Yes, he told me not to tell anyone about you, that you were in trouble. What's going on? Mo?" I could tell she was conflicted by fear of, and concern for me.

"I hope to god you're telling the truth." I said walking to the door. Mikayla raised palms as if to say what the fuck. "Let's roll."

In a flash the razor was in her hand. Piper froze.

"Step out of my way, Moses."

"No. We're done here."

"What? She batted her eyes and you bought her story?"

"Yup. Cut me or walk away." I balled up my fists. She would kill me no doubt, but I wasn't going to make it easy. Behind me, I could hear Piper gasp. The razor whipped up, stopped an inch from my eye.

"Is she worth an eye?"

"Yes."

"Fine." She held the blade for a moment then retracted it and folded it into her pocket. She walked out without looking back.

Piped leaned against the counter, breathing hard.

"I'm sorry, baby, I had to know."

"Fuck you, Moses, fuck you. I've never been anyplace but in your corner." She was looking at her feet.

"I know, but things are so sideways."

"Just leave, Moses. Don't come back." Walking out, I knew I had broken a cardinal rule, I had gone against my friend. Chosen fear over her.

In the car, I wanted to ask Mikayla if she would have cut me. But I know she would have. She was hard-wired for destruction. Instead, I asked her why she hadn't.

"Because she was telling the truth. I knew when I saw her looking at you with the razor to your eye. She loves you."

"Not anymore," I said, letting it sink into my bones.

Manny's Chrysler was the only car in the parking lot behind the club. I knew he'd be counting out the night's receipts, he never trusted anyone, not even me, to do the final count or the bank drop.

Sliding my key into the back door, I moved in quietly. Motioning for Mikayla to check the lap room, I checked the restrooms. The place was empty, which didn't surprise me, the cleaning crew didn't arrive until the next day and everyone else was long off the clock.

The office door was open a crack, leaking a sliver of light into the dark hall. As I moved toward the door, I pulled the Beretta from my waistband.

Uncle Manny looked up from behind his desk. His eyes widened only slightly, a mere flicker of panic crossed his face then was gone. "Keep your hands on the desk, Manny."

"The cash is in the bank bag," he said, trying to stare me down.

"You know why I'm here."

"Yes, to rob me, you ungrateful son of a bitch."

I slapped the pistol down across his face, opening a small gash in his cheek.

"Wrong answer," Mikayla said, flipping the razor open.

"You want to cut me? So what?" Manny looked at the blade like it meant no more to him than a toothpick.

"Glendale Adventist," I said to Mikayla, "Bed five fourteen. You'll find an Arab there. Kill him."

"Ok," Mikayla shrugged and headed out the door. She got all the way down the hall before Manny broke.

"Wait, Moses, wait. Call her back."

"I'm way past fucking around here, Manny."

"Call her back, I'll tell you what I know." His shoulders slumped and he was suddenly a sad old man. I let her get ten more paces before I finally called out.

Coming back into the office, she looked put out at not getting to kill anyone. She leaned against a credenza behind Manny, flicking the razor open and closed.

"Tell me about the Israelis," I ordered Manny.

"Who?" He looked genuinely confused.

"The motherfuckers you sent to waste me at the bus depot."

"No, I called Dimitri Petravich. Moses, you must believe I had no choice. They threatened to kill my family. You saw what they did to my nephew, I had no choice." Sweat ran down his forehead.

"You always have a choice. You chose to give me up."

"I care for you like a son, if I thought they could succeed in harming you, I never would have told them. I knew you could take care of yourself, but my family..."

"You knew they had their girls whoring out of the club, didn't you?" I had to change the conversation away from his sentimental crap before I started believing him. "How did they get their hooks into you?"

"They threatened to have me sent down as a terrorist. They have friends working for Homeland Security. All they need is a suspicion and I would disappear. Guantanamo, Spain, wherever they were hiding combatants. I would be gone. Who would care for my family? What was the harm? A man wants to get his cock sucked, a girl is willing to suck it, what is the harm?"

"The girls weren't willing," Mikayla said. Manny turned around to look at her. Slamming my fist on the desk, I caught his attention. I had to keep him from engaging Mikayla and getting his throat slit.

"Bullshit, Manny. Some Russian gangster tells you he has government connections and you roll over? Nah, don't buy it."

"A federal agent came to the club, he said it was a routine immigration check. But I knew it was a message from the Russian. He was proving his connections were real. I'm not proud of what I did, but it was what I had to do. Now if you are going to kill me, please make it look like robbery so my wife can collect the insurance."

"You fucked me hard and dry, Manny. Killing you won't even this score, not by a mile. No, you stay in play with these bastards. You're my inside man now."

I told him to keep his cell on, I'd be in touch. On the way out, I grabbed the bank bag. It was the price he'd pay for fucking a friend.

Manny had been the only father I had ever known. He was a hard, street fighting bastard. I had trusted him. My mistake.

We made it two blocks before the government car hit its siren and lights.

CHAPTER 18

"Where the fuck are the girls?" The fed's belly hung over a rodeo belt.

"At the mall?" It was stupid, but fuck it, I was tired. I had been cuffed and on my knees for the past twenty minutes. The same question over and over.

Mikayla was gone. When he hit the siren, I jammed on the gas and let the beast roar. We hung a left so tight, I could feel the right tires lift off. He missed the turn but he wasn't far behind. Left, right, I was running blind through Frogtown, a small area of convoluted streets, pinned between the 5 and the LA river. The last turn was a mistake. Two hundred feet down, it dead-ended into the river. Slamming on the brakes, I gave Mikayla the cash, the Beretta and the name of the motel. Then I jumped out and ran towards the black sedan. Mikayla slipped into the shadow.

"Stuck your dick in a hornets' nest this time, boy." I could smell bourbon on his breath as he leaned into me. "I'm tossing you a life line, maybe you should think about taking it."

"Meet you halfway?"

"That's all I'm asking."

"Only one problem, chief."

"What might that be?"

"I have no fucking clue what you're talking about." He hit pretty good for an old guy. I fell over on my side.

"I'm sorry, damn my temper. Damn." Lifting me back onto my knees, he started to dust me off. Something hard hit something soft. His body went rigid. His hands stopped moving. He hit the pavement with a thud.

Mikayla stood over him, a bloody brick in her hand.

Harry Clemmit, that was his name, or at least that was what his ID said. He was a Federal Marshal assigned to Homeland Security. He had eight hundred and forty-two dollars, a VIP card from Fantasia's bikini club and not much else. He was handcuffed on the bed with a towel full of ice on his head. Mikayla sucked on a cigarette. I sucked on a Coke, wishing it was a scotch.

I had chosen the Rose Motor Lodge in Eagle Rock. They took cash and didn't ask any questions. It was a small court of pre-war single story bungalows. His wallet and half-drunk quart of Four Roses whiskey sat on the coffee table. His Remington 12 gauge and Kevlar vest rested by the door. His .44 Bulldog was in my belt.

Harry's lids slid open when we dumped an ice bucket full of cold water on him. Eyes darting, he tried to place himself. Navigating his way back from whatever dark place he had been, he locked on me.

"You are one sad sack dumb fuck, convict. Kidnapping a cop?"

"You look up my record?" I sipped the Coke.

"Two time loser, yeah, I looked you up. I got a sack of hammers at home that are smarter than you." He tried to sit up, pain swimming, he leaned back down.

"This here is strike three, the big bitch. I have nothing to lose by killing you." Another sip.

"Kill a cop, ride the needle. Is that what you want, son?" He was fighting his ornery nature to try and sound warm and fatherly. "I figure maybe I can help straighten this out, if you give me the chance. Un-cuff me, put our heads together, see what we see."

"I don't think so." Setting down the Coke, I pulled the .44. He relaxed, it was as if he had seen this moment coming a long time back and he was almost relieved to finally have it here. Pushing the barrel against his head, I pulled the trigger.

The hammer fell on an empty chamber with a hollow click.

Harry was in the trunk as we drove across town. The empty gun trick had opened the floodgates of truth. He was on the pad to the Russians. He had convinced his bosses they could help him fight terrorists, that was all it took to give him free rein. Mention the T word and nothing else mattered. The Israelis worked for Mossad. The Russian mob funneled them cash. Cash used to fight terrorists. Again the big T. He told me the Israelis had Gregor and Anya held in a safehouse in Chatsworth. That's where we were headed.

Back in the motel, I had cleaned my shoulder. Whatever Adolpho's woman had used had done the trick, the flesh was purple with bruising but no sign of infection. I turned the shower to scalding and let the water pound down on me. I hurt from head to toe and the water did little to ease it. What I needed was a week in bed. What I got was a head full of broken glass and rusty nails. Jason B. Manny. Piper. Faces flooded my mind. So many friends lost. It had started with a simple lap dance, and a girl I fell for. That was a life ago. Now she and my last friend were both in the hands of killers and it was on me to get them back.

"These men are very good at what they do, very good," Mikayla said as we purred up the freeway.

"Fuck them." I didn't look at her, we hadn't spoken ten words since we left Piper's.

"Look, I'm..." She was stumbling and unsure. "I'm, I didn't mean to... Your friend, the stripper..."

"Her name's Piper."

"Yes, Piper... Sometimes, I wish it was all different. Not sometimes. No, always I wish, but this is who I am." She went silent, eyes on the hills sweeping past us. Whatever fantasy I had in the desert was gone. Mikayla wasn't ever going on a date. She wasn't the kind of girl you took walking on the beach at sunset. The place those possibilities lived had died in her miles back down her twisted road. Maybe they had died for me, too, only I was too thick to admit it.

The sun was cresting the mountains as the new day broke over Chatsworth, redneck hell. Home of the peckerwood jury who kicked free the cops who beat Rodney King and set off the LA uprising.

At a filling station, I called Manny. He was still at the club. "Call the Russians. Ask them what it will take to get Gregor back."

"It may take time, where are you?"

"I'm at the Rose Motor Lodge, call me when you reach them." I gave him the number and hung up. From the parked car, I could see the dirt road Harry had mapped for us. The convenience store coffee tasted bitter. We watched the road. We waited.

Ten minutes later, a white van rolled down the mountain. We ducked down as they flew past us and onto the freeway. Manny had sold me out again. I knew he would. I was past caring. One day I might kill him, but not this day.

"I need a drink," Harry said when we opened the trunk. His face was a bit red, but other than that, he looked better than when we shoved him in there. "Goddamn, convict, I'm six feet down and waiting for the dirt. Give me a drink or shoot me." His hands, cuffed behind his back, were starting shake with building tremors.

Unhooking the cuffs, I handed him the Four Roses. He sat up in the trunk, back pressed against the inside of the fender, and took one long pull off the bottle.

"You ever listen to Dolly Parton?" He hit the bottle again.

"I hate country music."

"Your loss, convict, your loss." His trembling stopped

with the whisky. Climbing out he looked up the dirt road. "Sure you want to do this? These are some mean mother truckers."

"Let's go."

"It's your neck and your razor." He led us around the bend. At the end of the dirt road, a Quonset hut sat surrounded by oaks and scrub. Mikayla circled around the back, through the trees. I gave her a few minutes before moving to the front door. Pinning myself against the wall, I leveled the 12 gauge at Harry's chest. His fist pounding on the metal door echoed into the quiet morning. Heavy footsteps on concrete. The peephole darkened.

"Open up, the Russkies sent me, we got trouble." Sweat beads popped on Harry's forehead. A steel bolt slid and the door started to open. Shoving Harry aside, I slammed into the door. It flew open, the man behind it was quick, instead of toppling, he used my force to propel himself into the shadows. I was stumbling into the room when he fired the first burst. Flame jumped out of the darkness. The doorway I had been in was filled with the buzz of lead. Falling to my belly, bullets ripped holes of light into the wall behind me. Aiming at the flame, I pulled the shotgun's trigger. It slammed into my fucked up shoulder, sending shivers of pain with every shot. I pulled the trigger as quick as I could, the Remington's smooth auto load kept the shots coming. I didn't stop until the breach locked open. All went silent. Dust motes and gun smoke drifted in the shafts of light piercing in through the bullet holes. Setting the Remington down, I pulled my Beretta and crawled towards the shadowed form. Buckshot had taken the Israeli's head off at the jaw line. Bloody pulp smeared the wall behind him. I swallowed and kept moving.

Stepping into a back room that had been converted into

a kitchen, I slipped on something wet and almost fell. The floor was slick with blood. A man lay on his side, his hands locked on his throat where he had unsuccessfully tried to stop his life from flowing out of a razor cut.

Through a door on the left, I found Mikayla leaning over Gregor. In the small windowless room, he sat on the floor. She cut the plastic cuffs off his hands and feet. When she pulled off the hood covering his face, he blinked against the light, then looked up at me.

"How's it going, boss?"

"Been better, you?"

"Been worse." Standing up, he almost fell over, grabbed the wall for support.

"Sit." In the corner, I found his clothes. I pulled on his jeans as gently as possible, he didn't scream but I could tell he wanted to. Bruises, gashes and rips left no part of his body unharmed. I had to cut the top off his left boot to fit it on over his broken toes.

"Sorry, I shouldn't have dragged you into this."

"Fuck it, boss, comes with the job." When he smiled, I saw he was missing a tooth and two others were chipped. "You get Anya?"

"No." I couldn't look him in the eye.

"Then what the hell are we waiting for. That white haired old fuck took her." He was pulling on his shirt and hobbling for the door.

"You need a hospital, kid."

"Fuck that, boss. What I need is to kill some Russians."
Stepping past the bloody mess in the kitchen, he spat on the
dead body. A tarot card lay on the guy's chest.

Mikayla met us on the way out with a filled army blanket
slung over her shoulder like some dark version of Santa Claus.
Gregor grunted and nodded his head at her.

"She's with us," I told him, and that was all he needed. I
was stepping out the door when Mikayla grabbed my arm.

"What?"

She pointed down. A foot off the floor, a piece of fishing
wire was drawn taut. It ran through an eyehook and to the pin
of a hand grenade that she had strapped to a five gallon gas tank.

"You've been busy."

"Had to do something while you two were playing dress
up."

"I like her, boss, she's got balls."

"Yes, she does." Careful not to blow us up, I stepped out
the door, the daylight blinding me for a moment. I almost
tripped over Harry. He was curled onto his side. Bullets had
stitched a line across his gut. His eyes stared up dully.
Whatever he had deserved, I doubted it was to die in the hills of
Chatsworth.

I helped Mikayla lift him into the Quonset hut. I tucked
the near empty Four Roses bottle under his arm. Where he was
going, I figured he'd need a drink.

CHAPTER 19

Gregor was stretched out in the back seat, head lolling, eyes closed. Mikayla sat beside me, her bundle on her lap. A thin electronic version of Queen's *We Will Rock You* drifted into the car.

"Your blanket's calling."

"If I answer, they'll know something is wrong."

"Then don't answer it." We were treated to two more bars of Queen done badly before it clicked over to voice mail. Mikayla dropped the cell phone back into her pile of booty. At a quick glance, I could see wallets, a laptop, several manila folders, a watch and who knew what else. The woman was a scavenger, a vulture who survived off carrion. But who was I to judge. After loading Gregor into the car, I had gone back and collected all the guns and ammunition I could find. Her skill with a razor had blinded her to the fact that for where we were going, we would need firepower.

"Jesus H Christ, what happened to you?" Helen stood

in the door of her Silver Lake hillside home.

"Ran into some folks who didn't like the cut of our jib."

"Goddamn it, Moses, don't. This is way past funny, Ok? I write about vampires and gangsters for the WB, I don't know how to... shit, Moses, shit."

"Can we come in?"

"Yes, damn you, yes."

Gregor stumbled under his own steam over to the sofa and dropped down. Helen looked him over, shaking her head. "He needs a doctor."

"No he doesn't," Gregor said.

"The girls?" I asked.

"Downstairs, poor little things." I nodded to Mikayla, who set down her bundle and headed for the stairs.

"No you don't, not before you wash the blood off your hands and face. Those girls have seen enough horror shows for this lifetime." She got Mikayla a towel and showed her to the bathroom. Coming back, she looked worried.

"Nice company you're running with."

"Where's Peter?"

"Locked up in my office, typing, calling. I haven't seen him take a bite or a crap since they got here." Dark circles ringed her eyes. I wished I could make it all go away. I wished I had something to say, but I was all out of sorrys.

Peter's head snapped up when I entered. His eyes were black pin points surrounded by red. The shades were drawn and the only light was from the computer screen. In a machine gun rant, he told me of the article he was writing. His editor was holding a front page slot for him. This was going to blow the fucking top off those slave dealing bastards. He was sure once the story broke, the state department would have to give the girls asylum. He had reached out to a woman from the Angel Coalition, and another from Stop The Slavery. They would help the girls get a fresh start.

When I gave him the laptop and files, told him about the Israeli connection, he leaned back, rubbing his eyes.

"This is big times ten, damn... Are you sure, Mossad? Rogue or not, doesn't matter, right? They're here on US soil. Big. Let me see, um, yeah." He flipped open the laptop and hit a few keys. Then slammed it shut. "Fuck, encrypted, fuck. No worry, I know a guy knows a guy. Yeah, alright." I left him poring over the manila folders.

The sound of Russian voices led me out onto the lower deck. The girls looked fresh and clean, and if not happy, at least human. Nika turned to me, in a large tee shirt and sweat pants she looked thirteen years old. I looked away.

"I am glad you did not die." She craned her neck, looking up at me.

"The day's young."

"My sister, she is?"

"Soon. Trust me." I ran back upstairs, bile backing into my throat. All I could see was my dick in her.

I left the girls to Mikayla, who was trying to find out if

they knew anything that might help us track down the Russians. On the way over, we had cruised the West LA mansion only to find it empty and abandoned.

Upstairs, I found Gregor with a monstrous turkey sandwich in one hand and the stolen cell phone in the other.

"You want to reach out and talk to that Russian bastard?"

"You found his number?"

"Dumbfuck didn't clear his voicemail. The old man sounded real pissed to hear you had made it back to LA." Some of the color had returned to Gregor's face. Son of a bitch looked like he might actually survive.

Ten minutes of dialing proved the Russians smarter than I had thought. The phones had all been disconnected. Peter's contacts discovered squat, the numbers all linked to prepaid dump phones.

Uncle Manny hadn't left his office. Gray stubble patches dotted his chin. He looked sunken and old as dirt. He showed no surprise when I stepped in.

"How many times do you think you can sell me out before I put one between your eyes?"

"You will do what you must, as I have."

"I used to look up to you. When did you become such a pussy?"

"You get a family, build a life, care and feed it. You have nothing, you have no idea what you would do to keep it safe."

"Sold your soul for the rose garden, huh? Fuck you, Manny. You don't think I have shit I care about? I have a life, old man. I want it back."

"I don't think that this is possible."

"Then we're both fucked. Call the Russians, tell them I want out."

"It won't be easy."

"Neither is dying. Make the call."

Manny left a message at their drop line, he told them I was there and needed to speak to them. After that, we had nothing to do but wait. Any anger I had for the old man was gone, replaced with sadness.

Behind us, the strip club sat empty. The scent of lust, sold out rain checks and broken promises permeated the stained carpet and soiled booths. How many men had busted a nut in the lap room hoping to feel alive, only to leave more hollow then when they came in? How many girls traded their joy for cynicism, one buck at a time? Burn the fucker to the ground. The price paid for this shit was way too high.

The phone rang like a gunshot to my head. Manny played it straight. Told them I wanted out. Told them he thought I was finished, ready to deal.

"He wants to speak to you." He passed me the receiver.

"What?"

"And a good day to you, too, Mr. McGuire. You are a resilient termite, chewing at my structure, destroying so much of my life's work. In light of your imminent extermination, you want to deal?"

"I want my woman back and you out of my life. Do that and I'll let you get back to business."

"Bygones will be bygones, this is your deal? I lose my property, my pride and it costs you what? Nothing? No. Here is my counter offer. Bring me the girls, all of them, and I will afford you twenty-four hours to leave the country."

I hung up the phone.

"Time for you to blow town, Manny."

"What did he say?"

"Forget him. I'm retiring you. Take your family, find a small town where I won't have to see you. We clear on this?"

"Yes."

Walking through the club, I fought the urge to set a match to it.

The noon sun burned onto the back parking lot as I descended. The daylight showed the club in all its shabby glory. Purple paint blistered and peeled on the stairs. I was unlocking the Crown Vic's door when a shadow fell across my back. A huge form reflected in the window. I dropped down. A massive fist swung over my head, smashing the glass where my head had been.

Pasha the giant towered over me. I swung up, my fist bounced ineffectually off his gut. It was like hitting an iron plate. His fist flew down towards my face. Rising, I took the blow on the chest. I bounced off the door, leaving a dent. I gasped for air that wouldn't come. Meat paws grabbed my shoulder, lifting me to my feet. His arm cocked back, ready to take my head off.

"Blin! He needs to tell us where the girls are." A pale hood held Pasha's hand back. It took a lot for Pasha not to swing. This was what he was built for. Slowly, the tension left his face.

"Where are they?" The pale boy pushed a pistol barrel into my crotch, snapping back the hammer. The blade made no sound cutting through his throat. His blood splashed down onto my face. The man fell, revealing Mikayla standing behind him, the wet razor in her hand. Pasha stood stone still. Gregor pressed the shotgun barrel into the back of his head.

"Dude, please, tell me where they're holding Anya. If I take the leash off my girl, it will get messy, and I've had enough blood to last a lifetime." We were parked on a quiet dirt road in Griffith Park. Pasha hadn't said word one since leaving the parking lot.

"Fuck it, boss, time to start taking souvenirs." Gregor hobbled over to the front of the car, using a shotgun for a cane. Pasha was bound, leaning against the hood, his eyes bored. Gregor flipped the gun up by the barrel. The butt broke Pasha's lip and I could hear teeth snapping off.

"Chill." I pushed Gregor back, he was getting ready to hit the Russian again.

"Fuck that, Mo, he knows where Anya is."

Mikayla had her back to us, smoking. All this talk made her uncomfortable. Cut him and be done, was her plan. Always.

"I'm telling you, big man," I said, moving between Pasha and the mad Armenian, "I can't hold this shit together much longer. Just tell me where she is. You walk, Anya walks, happy fucking ending."

"Nyet."

"You speak, that's something."

"No happy ending."

"Yeah, you're right. Maybe just a less ugly ending. Could we try for that?"

He closed his mouth into a tense bloody line.

"Enough talk." Mikayla lifted her freshly cleaned razor and walked toward the giant.

"No, cut him one tiny bit at a time, turn him into so much ground chuck and he still won't talk. Trust me."

"We'll see." She raised the blade, resting it against his ear.

"I've run out of options, or I'd never ask you to do this." Nika studied my face. The other girls were in Helen's living room watching MTV and eating Spaghetti-Os.

"Will this get my sister back?"

"I don't know, but it's what I got."

She nodded her head and followed me into the garage. Pasha was trussed up in the back seat. It took some pleading but Mikayla and Gregor had been convinced not to take him apart one piece at a time. I had lost some tough guy points in their eyes, but fuck it, I was too tired of destruction to care.

Moses closed the car door behind Nika and stepped away, leaving the teenage girl alone in the back seat with the giant. For a long moment, they stared at each other.

When she finally spoke, it came out as a whisper. "My name is Veronika Kolpacolva, I come from Yaroslavl. All I wanted were pretty clothes, a house with a swimming pool. That was forever ago. My sister is a good woman, she's not trash to be thrown away. You are not trash. I need you to remember, please, remember. Once you were young and hoped life would be more."

Pasha looked at this little girl. When had life gotten so ugly?

"Tell me where my sister is. I need her to be alive and safe. You can be a hero instead of this. Be a hero. Save my sister."

I stood in the shadows of the garage, watching Nika. She was brave beyond her years, after all that men had done to her, she had the courage to sit in the car with this giant. I could barely hear her murmured Russian. After what seemed like forever, the giant spoke. Nika nodded her head. They spoke more. She leaned up and kissed his cheek.

"Here." Nika handed me a slip of paper. "They are holding Anya there. Get her back." The young bend but don't break easily. Old fucks like me, that's a different story.

Peter printed a map off the computer, the address was in Redlands, tucked between the Santa Ana river and the foothills of the San Bernardino mountains.

"You coming with us? See how it all ends?"

"My guy's guy almost cracked the laptop. The wire's crackling with an explosion in Chatsworth, bodies found. The story goes to press Friday. I'm up to my ass in fact-checking."

"I wasn't going to let you come anyway. Someone has to survive to tell the tale."

When I returned to the garage, Mikayla was in the front passenger seat. Gregor was in the back. "Not this time, Gregor, I want you to sit this one out."

"No."

"Pal, look in the mirror. You're done."

"They have Anya." Something in the way he said her name told me all the talk in the world wouldn't get him out of the car.

"Where's the big Russian?" I asked Mikayla, sliding in behind the wheel.

"The trunk."

"Alive?"

She looked at me like I was an idiot child. I wanted to ask her why, but I knew her answer, we had what we needed and he was one less scumbag on the planet. I hoped she was wrong, hoped that redemption was possible, but I suspected she was right.

CHAPTER 20

It was still early enough to avoid the parking lot the 10 became after quitting traffic. Gregor sat rigid, the mixture of Helen's Percodan and Peter's coke had taken his pain and sealed it into a soft little lock box.

"Put these on." I passed him a pair of Ray-Bans. His crazy eyes were more than I needed to see.

Mikayla was counting out a fat wad of cash. She had given the wallets and documents to Peter. The cash and jewelry were her spoils.

"When this is over, where will you go?"

"It is never over."

True for her, not for me. I was done, fried and baked. My life up to this point had been one long battle and I was ready to see it end. The citizens with their nine to fives looked real good.

This was bad.

Tired and weak was a quick way to get dead. Anya was

out there, waiting. Nika was counting on me to save her sister. I owed her, hell, more than I could repay.

It was Clash time. Crank up the guitars. Turn the stereo to attack. Mikayla cringed at the sound, but said nothing.

"Give me a line," I barked at Gregor. Dumping a fatty on the top of my hand, I took a blast. It was alligator heart time. Dump rage on top of the machine gun heartbeat. Angel, my beautiful pup, was still touch and go, the vet didn't give her good odds. Fuckers have to die. Anya, her lips on mine, could have been true love, they fucked that. Her tears. Nika's broken cherry, her blood on my cock. Mikayla's severed breast. Fuck fuck fuck. Ahhhhhh!

My scream rose above *The Last Gang In Town*. In the rearview, Gregor grinned. He might not walk real good, but he was ready to take some heads.

Xlmen lay on his belly, in amongst the white sage he was all but invisible. Ripping a piece of deer jerky, he kept his eyes on the ranch. It had taken him a long day to discover that the gringo had been driven to Tecate. Bodies in the borderland had been found with the bitch's cards. He had lost their trail in the southern tip of the Mojave. In the two days since crossing the border, he had followed the Russian. He figured they would not let what happened in Ensenada rest. Sooner or later, they would go for the big gringo and the tarot bitch or, the two would come for the Russians. Either way, he would be waiting. Señor Santiago had instructed him to let the assassin be, she was gone and that was all he wanted. A weak move. He had been sent to kill her. And he would. If he let this bitch best him, what would come next? He could feel the breath of old age tracking him, getting closer. He knew if he fell, the young street dogs would feast on his bones. His reputation was all that kept the curs at bay.

"Nailing yourself some midweek poon, huh?" The gap toothed clerk winked. After drifting in the foothills for forty lost minutes, I had pulled into a Stop-N-Shop for directions.

"If you say so." The coke had my teeth grinding.

"Ain't nothin' to be ashamed of, no siree Bob. Man has a right to get his dick wet without needin' to buy a girl no diamond ring."

"How do I get there?" I was making a real effort not to reach over the counter and pinch his skinny neck.

"In a hurry, yup, know that feeling. Dang, they got some girls out there will wring the wiggle out of your worm. Call me a liar if it ain't true."

I was seconds away from calling in Mikayla and letting her get him to talk when he finally gave up the directions.

Rolling off the highway, we moved down an unmarked gravel road. The headlights pierced the black. No moon or streetlights. River stones the size of Volkswagens lined our way. Cresting a rise, a farmhouse glowed in the distance. I killed the lights and slowed to a crawl, keeping us on the road as much by feel as sight.

Wooden horse fences surrounded several acres of pasture, a freshly painted farmhouse and a barn that looked one good gust of wind away from falling over. From the sage a hundred feet above the ranch, I watched. Floodlights on the house and barn lit the surrounding area, no one was going to sneak up on them. Through the windows, people could be seen moving inside. Two men sat on the porch. One leaned on what looked like a rifle. In a corral behind the house were parked several Mercedes, a Suburban and a rusted GMC pick-up.

"What's the plan, boss?"

"Go in hard, come out alive."

"Works for me."

We finished the toot in two lines. Gregor crunched a Percodan and racked a shell into the Remington auto loader.

"Put this on." I tossed him the Kevlar vest I'd taken from the dead fed.

"You put it on."

"I can run, can you?"

"Yes," he lied. Pain in the ass.

"Put it on or I dump you here, let the coyotes have you."

"Whatever, boss." He shrugged into the vest.

Opening the trunk, I was confronted by the dead giant. His neck had been broken. Whatever his plans for the coming year, he wasn't going to get to them. Fuck him, he chose the life. Pushing him to the side, I got to the guns we'd pilfered from the Israelis. I stuffed a Jericho .45 auto into my belt and the Beretta into the opposite side. Harry's short barreled .44 went into my jacket pocket. I hung the strap of an Uzi around my neck.

"Got enough guns?" Mikayla stubbed out a cigarette.

"I doubt it."

I keyed the Crown Vic to life and mashed down the accelerator. The V8-driven monster spat dust and gravel out the back as we soared toward the light. The boys on the porch jumped up as we splintered the gate. I was passing sixty MPH when I hit the E-brake, and racked the wheel to left. We slid sideways towards the porch. A shotgun boomed from the back seat. A painful ringing filled my ears. I fought to stop the beast before we collided with the house.

Shafts of light bore down through the dust storm we caused. The skid hadn't ended before Mikayla was out the door and on the run around the building. From the second story, I saw the rapid flash of automatic fire. Bullets ripped through the car's roof, tearing up the seat beside me. Rolling out the door, I put the car between me and the guns in the house. I thought Gregor would follow. The shotgun report told me he didn't. Opening the back door, he sat with his back to me, firing up at the house. A manic grin was glued to his face. Never give drugs to an amateur.

A fresh burst ripped through the headliner. These fuckheads were doing a real job on my ride. Grabbing the scruff of Gregor's jacket, I dragged him out the door. From the ground, he looked up at me like I was the asshole.

And that was when the shit got bad.

From the house, bullets punched ugly holes into the Crown Vic. From out of the barn, I saw a flash just before the dirt by my face exploded. We were trapped in the crossfire. Any way we went was death. The next bullet grabbed a piece of my leather jacket, pulling it open. Gregor, still grinning like an idiot, slipped fresh shells into the Remington.

I flicked my eyes up over the car to the house. He nodded.

Gripping the Uzi, I rolled into a crouch, leapt up and started to run toward the barn. Behind, I heard the shotgun; Gregor was firing over the hood of the car into the house. I hoped he could keep them from shooting me in the back.

I got twenty feet before the first bullet hit me. Flame popped from the barn. There were at least two shooters. I felt the hot burn along my lower left side. The Uzi jumped in my hand. One quick bone-rattling burst and it was empty. Thirty-two shots in a blast. I barely hit the broad side of the barn, but it had driven the shooters for cover and bought me ten feet free of their fire.

Dropping the Uzi, I pulled my Beretta and dropped to one knee. Aiming up at the door, I was ready when the bastard poked his head out. He was dressed in night camo and leveling a sniper's rifle when I took off the top of his head.

Bursting through the barn door, I almost killed Mikayla. She was standing over a second Israeli in camos. He was wet and still.

"Looks like your trip wire didn't take them all out."

"They are dead now." No smile. No pride. Just a fact.

Out the barn door, I watched, helpless, as Gregor fell. Bullets rained from the second story window. He slumped down behind the car.

Picking up the Israeli sniper's rifle, I wrapped the strap around my forearm, just as Uncle Sam had taught me. Clicking the sight in, adjusting for distance, bullet drop, wind, I let the cross-hairs drift across the upper window. A man leaned out, searching the ground below for his shot at Gregor. His blonde hair was tousled, as if he had been woken from a restless sleep. In the scope, I could see his pale blue eyes. He was young. I let out a breath and pulled the trigger. A pink puff danced off his head. And he was dead. His eyes would haunt me later. But not then. Then, it was killing time.

Swinging the sights onto the next window, I waited, stilling my coke driven heart. A shadow moved behind a curtain and I fired. The bullet shattered the glass and flapped the curtain open long enough for me to see a tall man fall. I scanned the front of the ranch house but nothing moved. Dropping the rifle, I noticed Mikayla had disappeared.

When I got to Gregor, his breath was shallow. Blood streaked his left arm and he was missing his two middle fingers. Ripping his shirt, I wrapped a tourniquet on his arm. The vest was pocked with lead. His eyes fought to focus.

"I fucked her, boss." His voice was a thin whisper.

"I figured."

"I love her."

"I figured that, too."

His eyes drifted closed.

It was time to end this shit.

I stepped over the twisted bodies of the men Gregor had killed on the porch and kicked open the front door. A fat older man sat on the floor, holding a bleeding gut. He struggled to raise the pistol in his hand. I emptied the Beretta into him.

From the back of the house, I heard the gurgled gasp of a man with a slit throat.

Dropping the Beretta, I pulled the Jericho .45 and moved up the stairs. The landing led to a hall with doors on both sides. Red numbers had been painted on each door.

Behind door number one, a naked man with a farmer's tan crouched behind the bed. He was holding a naked girl in front of him. One fist held her hair, in the other was a pocket knife, pressed to her chest, ready to plunge.

"Let me walk or I swear I'll kill her."

The slug entered his left eye and sprayed his skull across the wall. Dumb fuck John. As he flopped down, I recognized the screaming girl.

"Marina?"

She was way past realizing who I was. She just kept staring at the dead man and shrieking.

Doors two and three only held more panicked girls.

Door four was empty.

From downstairs, I heard a gunshot, only one. Odds were, Mikayla had ended it.

Pulling open door five, I was met by the burst from an AK. The doorjamb beside me shattered, spraying splinters and plaster into my face. The pain was distant, dulled by the coke numb. Dropping to the floor, I aimed up. I had to shake my head to clear the blood from my eyes.

Victor didn't look so good, a cast covered one arm, a bandage was wrapped around his head and velcro held a brace to his leg. He should have stayed in the hospital. With his good arm, he tried to bring the AK down. Surprise flooded his face when my first slug caught his chest and pushed him into the wall. I'll give him credit for balls, he still fought to get the rifle sighted in on me. I squeezed the trigger until the slide locked open.

Stumbling down the hall, I found the only door without a number. I put my boot to it. On the bed, Anya lay motionless. The white haired old man sat in a chair beside her. The silver revolver in his hand was pointing at me. The hammer was back. I held the .44 low, from the hip. I might hit him, might hit her.

"Look, my dear, your Galahad has breached the walls." Anya's limp form didn't move when he spoke to her. "Shall we pull the triggers and see who walks out of this room?"

"Why the fuck not." I fired wide, his eyes looked surprised. He hadn't expected me to actually do it.

As the bullet ripped the wall above him he pulled the trigger. Flame leapt from his hand toward me. Pain burned in my chest where the bullet ripped at my flesh.

I dove at the old man, landing before he could get a second shot off. Toppling body on body. The chair collapsed beneath our weight. I could feel the revolver pinned between us, he was struggling to pull the trigger. My fingers locked around his wrinkled neck. The fine bones in his throat broke with a sickening crackle. His body went slack, defeat filled his eyes. A spasm wracked his body as it fought for air that wouldn't come. His eyes bugged, went bloodshot, and then he was gone. I rolled onto my back and waited for death to take me.

Opening my eyes, a blurry Valkyrie kneeled over me. Valhalla couldn't be far off.

"What are you grinning about?"

"Fuck, I thought I was dead." It burned to speak.

"You're not that lucky." It was one of the few times I'd seen Mikayla smile.

"Is she dead?" Crawling to the bed, I looked down at Anya.

"Drugged. Strong pulse."

Anya was so beautiful. I could see her on stage, that first time, so solid, so real. Now here we were. In the middle of all that blood and death. I knew now that I didn't love her. Never had, really. What I fell for was the possibility of her and who I might be with her. I fell in love with my reflection in her eyes. Had she played me to get her sister back? Hell yes. But I went willingly. If Gregor survived, she would be with him, if he didn't, she would find another. I had stepped too far off the map to ever be with a woman like her.

Mikayla looked from the sleeping girl to me and said, "You and me, we plant trees we'll never be allowed to enjoy the shade of."

"Ukrainian proverb?"

"African." She dropped a card on the dead old man and helped me to my feet. "Can you walk or do I have to carry you?"

"Screw that noise." The walls swam around me as I fumbled my way through the house, using the walls for balance. Mikayla took up the rear with Anya over her shoulder.

Mikayla loaded Anya and Gregor into the back of a stolen Mercedes while I leaned on the porch. She was walking towards me when I heard the crack of a rifle. Blood blossomed on her chest. Her legs dropped from under her and she fell forward. She was dead before she hit the dirt. Standing up, I spread my arms wide and waited for the shot to come.

Long seconds past.

I dropped my arms.

CHAPTER 21

"Una mas cerveza?"

"Why not." I took the bottle from Adolpho and drank deep. Waves broke on the beach and out beyond the breakers, a school of dolphins danced under the clear blue sky. Jaquene, Adolpho's son, danced along the wet sand playing tug-of-war with Angel. She had recovered much quicker than me, I had to be careful not to give her any spicy foods, but other than that she had returned to her normal, sloppy self.

It had been six months since I had seen LA's broken skyline, I didn't miss the bitch, not much. The combination of beer and painkillers kept the ghosts at bay and allowed me some moments of peace.

I was in the hospital when Peter's story broke; the bastard used my name. I was famous for about fifteen minutes longer than I would have liked. On the upside, the notoriety kept the cops from digging too hard for evidence. And I got two hundred grand from some Hollywood slime ball for the movie rights. I used the cash to buy a small place down on the beach below Ensenada. With Mikayla's death, the local pimp's beef with me had ended. Business was business, I guess. Adolpho wept when he admitted it was he who told the hunter he had taken me to Tecate. His wife and kids had been on the line. I told him I would have done the same. It was a lie and he knew it. He and his son spend weekend days at my house, fishing, drinking beer and struggling through broken conversations. It feels right to be in a country without words. Few questions asked. No answers demanded.

Mikayla was the lucky one. Her painful run finally hit its end. I still see her in the corner of my vision, moving through the shadows. Two Percodans chased by cold Mexican beer sends her back into a dull fog of memory.

Gregor lost his arm, but the tough son of a bitch pulled through. Last I heard, he and Anya had taken her little sister and moved to Bakersfield. I hoped their house had a pool.

Piper called me in the hospital. She read the papers and said she understood why I had acted the way I did. But she didn't want to see me. She said I brought too much bad shit with me.

A British company bought Club Xtasy, I heard they made Doc the manager. And so it goes on. Little girls taking off their clothes for drunk men; all hoping for a transaction that won't leave them with less than they came in with. Not one of them clear-eyed enough to see that the price paid is never worth it.

COMING SOON

ONE MORE BODY – A Moses McGuire Novel.

Threatened with a life behind bars, Moses is reluctantly dragged back into war. The battlefield is the street. There is no DMZ. The 16ᵗʰ St. Titans take no prisoners and accept no surrender. Then again, neither does Moses McGuire.

Made in the USA
Charleston, SC
23 June 2011